THE SECRET OF HELENA'S BAY

Shelley Freeman travels to an idyllic Greek isle to recover from a broken romance. When elderly Stefan von Mueller disappears soon after speaking to her, she's drawn into a disturbing mystery. Everyone else at the resort, including handsome owner Paris Georgiadis, claims never to have seen Stefan. Shelley starts questioning her sanity, and then fearing for her life, as wartime secrets start to unfold. She soon wonders if she can trust Paris with her heart — and with her life . . .

SALLY QUILFORD

THE SECRET OF HELENA'S BAY

Complete and Unabridged

LINFORD
Leicester

First published in Great Britain in 2010

First Linford Edition
published 2011

British Library CIP Data

Quilford, Sally.
The secret of Helena's Bay. - -
(Linford romance library)
1. Missing persons- -Fiction. 2. Islands- -
Greece- -Fiction. 3. Romantic suspense
novels. 4. Large type books.
I. Title II. Series
823.9′2–dc22

ISBN 978-1–44480–530–7

Published by
F. A. Thorpe (Publishing)
Anstey, Leicestershire

Set by Words & Graphics Ltd.
Anstey, Leicestershire
Printed and bound in Great Britain by
T. J. International Ltd., Padstow, Cornwall

This book is printed on acid-free paper

1

The brochure said that the church in the mainland town was a 'must see', so instead of going directly to the islet of Agios Georgious — Saint George — the guests were taken straight from the airport to the church.

It had all the hallmarks of a Greek Orthodox church; pristine white stone and a blue dome, which appeared to become part of the blue sky above. The dome also emphasised the fact that darker clouds were coming in from the ocean. A storm was on the way. They had been told it would reach the islet by evening.

'The church was originally built in the twelfth century,' Annette, the holiday facilitator, said. 'But it has been added to considerably.' She pointed to a small doorway. 'That was the original entrance, and the wing behind it is the old church. As you can see, it was tiny. Not much bigger than a garden shed.'

'If your garden shed is in the grounds of Buckingham Palace,' a man called Len said sardonically. He was in his late fifties, with an arrogant swagger about him.

'The new entrance is on the left. Inside the modern wing there's a lot more room to move,' Annette continued in a patient tone.

Shelley broke away from the group and wandered from the blazing heat into the cool cloisters of the church. Even in the bigger wing, the arched stained glass windows were relatively small, presumably to keep out the midday sun. Light cast rainbow colours across the worn flagstones.

An elderly man sat in one of the front pews. When Shelley drew near, he looked up and smiled.

'It is magnificent, is it not?' he asked in a German accent, whilst gesturing towards a spot above the altar.

The main window, the one for which

2

the church was famous, was high above the altar table. It showed Saint George on a white charger. In one hand he held a sword, in the other a deep red rose, the glass of which cast refracted light onto the altar table.

'Yes, it's beautiful,' Shelley agreed.

'It is, isn't it?' Annette said, coming up behind Shelley and making her jump. 'It was restored by Yaya, who you'll meet at the islet. She's going to teach you to make stained glass.'

'I don't think I'll manage anything that beautiful,' Shelley said.

'No, probably not,' Annette replied. Her response was so blunt that Shelley winced. 'Come on, everyone,' Annette continued. 'I'm sorry to cut the visit short, but we're told the storm is heading this way much more quickly than we thought. We need to get you all on the ferry, otherwise we'll be spending the night on the mainland.'

Shelley looked around to where the old man had been sitting, intending to wave goodbye. He was gone, but a few pews back sat a younger man. His down-turned profile was in shadow, yet still she felt a small thrill, as if she instinctively knew he would be attractive. He had a definite presence in the way he held himself, even whilst seated. She had not realised she was staring at him until he looked around at her and smiled, showing his handsome face to the light.

Blushing a little, she followed the others out of the church and back into the blinding sunlight. She turned around to see if he was still sitting there or whether he was a part of the group. Her eyes had trouble focusing, but she was sure he had gone.

She looked for both men on the ferry over to the islet. Neither of them was on it. Which, she thought, was disappointing. Particularly where the younger man was concerned.

There was a group of archaeologists, led by an attractive German man of about forty. He looked the part, but his associates did not. Shelley supposed that not everyone could look like Indiana Jones. However, these people looked more like East End thugs. She mentally chastened herself for being so judgmental. After all, her own instincts had been proved to be unreliable in the all-too-recent past.

'We are digging for artefacts,' the group leader told Shelley, leaning on the rail nonchalantly whilst smoking a cigarette. 'As you can imagine, Fraulein, there are many treasures to be found in this cradle of civilisation.'

'It sounds fascinating,' Shelley said, not totally impervious to his confidence and good looks, despite suspecting that he knew exactly how attractive he was. 'Are you staying at the farmhouse?'

'No, which is a great regret to me now.' His dark eyes twinkled down at her. 'We are camping near to the dig. I think I am getting too old for such pursuits, but I like to be close to where I am working. So, alas, I will not be enjoying your charming company.'

'That's a shame.' He reminded her of

the type of German officer that used to feature in second World War films. The honourable one, from a noble family, who hated everything Hitler stood for and was only sitting out the war in a POW camp.

Looking around at her fellow holidaymakers, it seemed to Shelley that she was going to be the youngest, and by quite a few years.

* * *

There was hardly anyone at dinner. The two elderly ladies who arrived together, Mrs Caldicott and Miss Charters, shared a table, but everyone else dined alone. If anyone, either by design or accident, drew close to an occupied table, the diner looked up startled whilst the person approaching swerved suddenly, as if an invisible barrier had jumped up, stopping further progress in that direction.

The brochure had promised that all meals would take place on the terrace, but the violent storm put an end to that idea. It had also postponed the first demonstration on account of Annette being stuck over on the eastern side, where she had gone with the archaeology team to show them where they could set up camp. As there were no cars on the islet, her only way back was on foot. The guests were promised that she would return by the time dinner ended.

Shelley quite liked the dining-room. It was set out in rustic style, with candles in old wine bottles on the tables, and pictures of old farmland — presumably the islet in more verdant days — on the walls. It made her feel secure, as if there were somewhere she could hide in its thick stone walls, whereas outside she might have felt exposed, and not just to the elements.

She had spent far too much time indoors over the preceding months; too ashamed to show her face to the neighbours, so the idea of being outside for any length of time understandably made her feel a little nervous.

Mrs Caldicott and Miss Charters waved at Shelley as she entered the restaurant, beckoning her to their table. She shook her head and smiled, trying to indicate she did not want to put them to any trouble, rather than the truth, which was that she did not want or need company.

The buffet table ran along the length of the window, laden with yoghurt, baskets of fresh fruit, golden honey, Greek salad, lentils, chickpeas, bread, and for the non-vegetarians, fish, barbecued pork and chicken. Outside, black clouds moved across the sea like a thick blanket, but they brought chill rather than warmth. Shelley took some chicken and Greek salad before finding a table in a small alcove, away from the scrutiny of the other half dozen diners.

'They say that we won't be able to go to the mainland until it's over,' Mrs Caldicott said to no one in particular.

'What a pity,' Miss Charters replied. 'I so wanted to see the church again before we left. We were there for such a short time.'

'I'm sure the storm won't last all week, Minnie, dear.'

Shelley was disconcerted when someone appeared and sat down at her table, despite there being several empty tables left. She tried the startled look, but it clearly didn't work on the man, as he ploughed through the psychological barrier. He took the seat opposite her. It was then that she saw he was the elderly man from the church.

'Good evening, Fraulein,' he said.

Shelley guessed he had once been very handsome and tall, though age had caused his shoulders to stoop a little and broken veins to appear on his once sharp cheekbones.

'Good evening,' she said, relieved it was him. He felt like a kindred spirit, though she did not understand why. 'I hadn't realised you were staying here, too. I didn't see you on the ferry.'

'You English are very strange,' he said, seeming to ignore her comment.

'The way you all avoid each other.'

'We'll be best friends by the end of the week,' Shelley said, smiling.

'True, but you will not say a word to each other until Friday evening.'

Shelley laughed. He'd just described every holiday she had ever been on with fellow Brits.

'That's true. We are a bit stand-offish. And I'm afraid that I'm probably one of the worst culprits.'

'Then you and I shall not be, as you say, *stand-offish*. We shall be instant friends. My name is Stefan,' he said, holding out his hand. It trembled slightly and felt cold to the touch, though his manner was warm enough.

'I'm Shelley.'

'You are surely not on Saint George's Islet for your health? You are too young. Not like us . . . how do you say it? Old fogeys.'

Shelley shrugged and smiled, ignoring the question. Mrs Caldicott and Miss Charters had already pumped her for information on the trip over from the main island.

'What brings you here, Stefan?' Shelley asked.

'This islet was occupied by my country during World War Two, and my father was sent here with the occupying forces. I come to right his wrongs.'

'In what way?'

'You know, I am sure, of the Nazi government's vile scramble for loot?'

'Yes, Nazi gold is a popular subject on the History Channel.'

'My father was among those who helped with the looting. Allied forces shot him not long after he had stolen some jewels from the small church that used to be on the islet. No one knows where my father hid them.'

'So you've come to find them?' Shelley wondered whether Stefan's motives were entirely innocent. He seemed a decent enough man, but her trustworthiness radar was somewhat damaged.

'Yes, but not for myself. I only wish to return them to their rightful owners.

My father's shame burns in me. It may be hard for you to believe, but I want to recover my family's good name. We were a proud family, of noble birth, before that little despot turned us all into the world's favourite race of monsters.'

'How do you know where to start looking? The islet is small, but there's still several hundred square metres to cover.'

'My father wrote letters to my mother about his time here. I have been reading them, trying to pick up clues. Places he visited. Where he spent most of his time here. There is one place . . . '

Stefan stopped as Mrs Caldicott and Miss Charters got up to leave, passing by their table, discussing Andy Murray's chances at Wimbledon.

'Let's hope we get back in time to see the finals,' Mrs Caldicott said.

'I have bored you enough,' Stefan remarked after they had gone. He rose from his chair.

'No, I'm not bored at all. Please, sit down and tell me more.' She'd been sure she would hate it on the islet, and only came because her mother insisted she take a break, even offering to pay for it. So she had gone online and opened up Google Earth, clicking with her eyes shut at any part of the map she thought might be warm. At the first try she got Beirut, then Iraq, so she tried again and again until she found Saint George Islet and an information box came up about the creative arts weeks run here.

She was not sure whether she truly wanted to write, throw pots, or make stained glass, all of which were included in the activities, but she did want her mother to stop nagging her. Now a bit of Nazi intrigue enthralled her more than the idea of any of the classes.

'I'd like to hear more about your father and the hidden jewels,' Shelley urged. But Stefan was not listening. He stared at the doorway, his face becoming pale. But by the time Shelley turned around, whoever he was looking at had left. 'Do you know you're not the only

13

German here?' she asked. There's a professor . . . em . . . Grunwald, doing an archaeological dig.'

'I am afraid I must say goodnight,' Stefan said, looking paler still. 'It has been very pleasant to talk to you. Perhaps I will tell you more tomorrow.'

'You're not coming to the demonstration?'

'Yes, but I must rest now. I will speak to you about this again, yes?'

As he stepped forward, he tripped, grabbing the back of Shelley's chair and knocking her bag, which had been hanging from it, to the ground.

'Please, excuse me,' he said, when he restored his balance and returned her bag to her. 'I am not so steady on my feet these days.'

'Are you all right?' Shelley asked anxiously. 'You look pale. Please, sit down and rest awhile.'

'No, I have to leave now. Thank you for your patience and kindness, Fraulein.' With that he gave her a courtly bow, and left the dining room.

Later, with dinner out of the way, the dining room was cleared, and the chairs placed in a less formal circular arrangement for the demonstration. A gong called the guests, who had been sent to a sun lounge on the other side of the building for five minutes whilst the clearing up operation took place.

'Sun lounge is something of a misnomer,' Len said. 'They promised us sunshine — and just look at the weather.'

'That's hardly the organiser's fault,' Miss Charters said reasonably.

Shelley sighed inwardly. Len was clearly going to be whinger of the week. Not that she felt any more hopeful about her time here — but she at least managed to keep it to herself.

Despite their best efforts to sit separately at the demonstration, it appeared the staff had removed some dining chairs, leaving exactly twenty-two for the twenty guests and two

15

facilitators, leaving them little choice but to sit next to someone.

'Good evening,' Annette said. Her blonde hair was damp, and her face had a scrubbed clean look. 'I apologise for my lateness. I was showing Professor Grunwald where he could set up camp, and, as they say in cricket, rain stopped play. So I ended up walking back. Two miles in the rain. I don't envy the professor and his team, camping out this weather, but despite my offer of shelter, he insists they'll be fine.'

'Goodness gracious! In this storm?' Miss Charters said anxiously.

'It's been much worse than this on Agios Georgious Islet,' Annette said, waving her hand as if it were of little import. 'In 1945 there was a tremendous storm. It totally destroyed the old church.' She gave the impression that it would take much more than a storm to knock her down.

The mention of the war years reminded Shelley of Stefan. She looked around, but he wasn't among the guests. She wondered if he'd heard the gong calling them to the demonstration.

'Now, before I split you into groups and go through the schedule, I'm going to call the register,' Annette said. 'To ensure you've all made it from the mainland.'

As she read out their names, a man entered the room. His hair was also damp, but jet black. His blue eyes, vivid against honey-coloured skin, brought to mind the Mediterranean on a calm day. He sat in an empty seat. Whereas everyone else sat upright and rigid, he leaned back, crossing long legs encased in beige chinos. He looked at Shelley and smiled. He was the younger man from the church.

Shelley was so busy looking at him, she almost missed answering to her name on the register.

'Oh, Shelley Freeman. That's me,' she said, putting up her hand, then feeling foolish, bringing it straight back down. After all, they weren't in school.

17

The rest of the guests laughed, making Shelley blush even more.

'Thank you.' Annette smiled tightly, glancing proprietarily at the newcomer who'd taken Shelley's attention. Shelley wondered whether they were a couple.

Annette read through the rest of the list, and was about to close the register, when Shelley spoke up.

'What about Stefan? Did I miss his name?'

'Who?'

'Stefan? The elderly German man who sat with me at dinner.' She looked around at her fellow guests for confirmation, but they all looked at her blankly.

'There's no one called Stefan on this list,' Annette said.

'But he was here at dinner. He was talking to me. An elderly man, about six feet tall. He didn't seem very well.'

Annette looked at the list again.

'Nope. No one here of that name.'

'You saw him, didn't you?' Shelley asked Mrs Caldicott and Miss Charters.

'Well . . . actually,' Mrs Caldicott

18

said, 'we didn't, dear. We could hardly see you where you hid yourself away in that alcove.'

'But you passed by my table. He stood up. He tripped over, remember?'

'I'm afraid we didn't see him,' Miss Charters said. 'We were busy discussing that nice young Mr Murray, so we weren't really paying attention.'

'Perhaps it was a gatecrasher,' Len, who was sitting next to Shelley, said.

'Yes, it could be,' Annette said. 'We get a few cheeky sorts making their way over here in the day, then trying to pop in and use our buffet. We once found a stowaway in one of the empty huts.' Outside the farmhouse was a village of grass huts, used as accommodation by the more hardy guests.

'He didn't seem that sort of man,' Shelley said. 'He was very nice . . . ' She felt herself getting hot, especially when she realised the dark-haired man was watching her intently. 'He was also in the church today.' She looked to him for some confirmation, but he just shrugged.

19

'We don't have anyone here called Stefan,' Annette said. She slammed the register shut, as if that were the end of the matter.

It turned it out to be only the beginning.

As Annette talked the group through health and safety, Shelley's mind turned over and over, wondering who Stefan was, and why he was not listed amongst the guests.

'The bay on the eastern side of the islet is out of bounds to guests,' Annette was saying. 'Not only does the sea have dangerous undercurrents, but Professor Grunwald and his team are over there digging for religious artefacts, so in a day or two it will resemble a building site, with all the dangers inherent, such as falling masonry and deep pits. But fear not, we do have a nudist beach on the northern end of the islet which I'm sure you'll all find just as interesting.'

'It'll be just like being back at the Windmill,' Miss Charters said, drawing a laugh from everyone.

Annette smiled tightly again. Shelley wondered if the facilitator ever smiled easily about anything. She seemed pleasant enough, but there was a reserve behind her eyes, reminding Shelley of the headmistress at her old school who never quite seemed to like children.

The facilitator carried on with the health and safety regulations, explaining where the fire escapes were, what to do in case of emergency and how to stay safe in classes and when moving around the islet.

'I would advise you all to go about in pairs,' Annette said. 'We've never had a problem in the five years the resort has been active, but that's because the facilitators before me have been vigilant. You'll have noticed that down near the jetty are the remains of the village. Be careful in that area, as some of the buildings are still dangerous.'

'Will there be chance to go the mainland?' Mrs Caldicott asked.

'Hopefully once the storm is over,'

Annette said. 'The ferry leaves here twice a day. At noon and at six in the evening. It comes from the mainland at eleven in the morning and five in the evening. So you won't have much time over there, but it will be enough.

'We'd quite like to see the church again, you see,' Miss Charters said.

'There's enough time for that. Now.' Annette clapped her rather large hands together. 'It is my pleasure to hand you over to our activities facilitator, Paris Georgiadis. Paris?'

The hunk sat up straight, and smiled, showing his even, white teeth.

'Good evening, everyone.' Shelley had expected him to be Greek. Surprisingly he spoke with an English accent. 'Yes, my name is Paris,' he continued. 'Yes, it has been the bane of my life, and as a teenager I hated my parents for it. No, I'm not looking for my Helen. At this stage in my life I'd settle for a face that launched a couple of jet skis.'

Whilst everyone else laughed, Shelley

did not like the fact he was looking at her when he said it.

Annette stood up and stalked from the room. Clearly the jet ski joke did not even warrant a tight smile.

'This islet,' Paris said, 'was owned by my late father's family before the German occupation. There were several other thriving farms, and the village, which, as Annette has explained, is now in ruins. The building we're in was the main farmhouse, which has been added to over the years. After the war, politics got in the way — I shan't bore you all with the details, but suffice to say the government decided we had to reclaim it, and it has taken us until recently to achieve that aim. Years of neglect rendered the islet unfit for further farming, other than the smallholding we use to grow vegetables. So we decided to open it up to visitors, offering holistic breaks to the world weary. The aim of this demonstration, as well as Annette advising you of health and safety, is to introduce you all to each other. My mother is British, hence my accent, so I know that if we don't do something about it, you'll all avoid each other until Friday.'

Shelley smiled. That was exactly what Stefan had said.

'Mrs Caldicott and Miss Charters, would you mind if I separated you two ladies? Just for this the purpose of this task. Miss Charters, swap with Ms Freeman.' He proceeded to organise the group into pairs. 'The purpose of this task is that you all get to know each other. Don't worry, I'm not going to ask you to sing. Not yet. The singing class is on Wednesday, I believe. Simply talk to your partner for five minutes. At the end of that five minutes, I want you to know their names, their occupations, if they're married or single, where they're from, and what made them come to this storm-battered place.'

As if on cue, one of the doors to the patio was flung open by the wind, causing everyone to jump.

'Don't worry, folks,' Paris said

laconically. 'That'll just be our resident ghost, Dimitri.'

'Ghost?' Miss Charters gasped.

'I'm joking,' Paris replied, smiling. Yet as he stood up to close the door, Shelley was sure she saw several dark figures moving away from the building. She got up and walked to the window, but it was too dark to see anything. She shuddered.

'Are you cold, Shelley?' Paris asked, his voice gentle.

'No, I'm fine. I just thought I saw someone outside.'

'Not on a night like this, I'm sure.' His eyes searched her face. There was something unnerving about the way he looked at her. Not least because he had a habit of catching her looking at him.

For the next ten minutes the room was filled with the sound of conversation. It was muted at first, but gradually, as people began to relax, laughter could be heard.

'Are we ready?' Paris asked. 'I gave you all extra time since you seem to be getting on so well. We'll start with you,

Mrs Caldicott. Tell me all about Ms Freeman.'

'Oh! Very well,' Mrs Caldicott answered, as if caught off guard. 'I thought you'd have started at that end,' she said, gesturing to the four people on her right, who were nearest to Paris in the circle.

'That's the predictable way of doing things,' he said, humour in his blue eyes. 'What have you learned about Ms Freeman?'

'Hmmm,' Mrs Caldicott said, as if she had her own thoughts about the way things should be done. 'Young Shelley here works in a law centre in Derbyshire, though she's originally from Kent. She was going to be married, but that didn't work out.'

Shelley coloured up, hoping against hope that Mrs Caldicott would not tell everyone the truth, which she had somehow blurted out, finding the older woman very warm, not to mention very inquisitive.

Mrs Caldicott looked at her kindly, as

if reading her thoughts.

'She's come here in the hopes that her mother will stop nagging her about getting a life.'

'Tell me about it,' Paris said, smiling at Shelley. 'Shelley, what have you learned about Mrs Caldicott?'

'Mrs Caldicott's first name is Rachel, but people always call her Mrs Caldicott, and she prefers that until she gets to know people better. She's a retired librarian — so we have a lot in common regarding a love of books. I'm afraid we spent most of the time chatting about that.' Shelley shrugged apologetically. 'We both enjoy Lee Child's thrillers and want to marry Jack Reacher in our next lives.'

'Really?' said Paris, grinning. 'What else?'

'I do know that Mrs Caldicott was born and raised in north London,' Shelley went on. 'Her husband died several years ago . . .' Shelley hesitated, remembering the sadness in the lady's dark eyes when she recalled her late husband. Instinctively, she reached out and touched Mrs Caldicott's arm. 'And she hasn't found anyone to replace him.' Shelley paused for a while, because it seemed the fitting thing to do. 'She's here with her friend, Miss Charters, to embrace new experiences. She doesn't know what state her chakras are in, or where they are in her body, but was heartened by the idea this holiday would sort them out once and for all.'

'Oh, yes, we're experts at mending chakras here.' Paris smiled.

'How do you do that, exactly?' Len asked challengingly. 'Medicine?'

'No, we rely on the scenery and the peace and quiet,' Paris replied.

As he spoke there was a clap of thunder outside.

'Can I have my money back?' Len quipped.

'If you still feel the same by the end of the week, we'll talk.' Paris grinned. Shelley noticed that his gorgeous smile always came very easily.

The rest of the group were introduced by their partners. Miss Charters's story, as told by Len, was pretty much the same as Mrs Caldicott's. She, too, used to work in a library, and was there to get her chakras fixed, but unlike Mrs Caldicott, she had never married.

'She says she's still holding out for Al Pacino,' Len said, rolling his eyes heavenward.

'Aren't we all?' Shelley quipped.

'Won't that make Jack Reacher jealous?' Paris asked.

Len was an ex-policeman from Leeds. He was widowed, and living in a studio flat above his son's garage since he had been injured in a car crash. He had taken the holiday at the behest of his daughter-in-law.

'He thinks she just wanted him out of the way,' Miss Charters said, pursing her lips.

'It was her slipping a road map into my passport that did it,' Len said, laughing far too bitterly for it to be a real joke. Despite his joviality, Shelley suspected that he hated having to rely on his son.

2

By the time Shelley made her way up to bed, she convinced herself that Stefan had merely been a confused old man who had wandered into the house by accident. His stumble showed he was not entirely steady on his feet. Maybe his mind was just as muddled. Her grandmother had been the same before her death. She refused to believe Stefan was a gatecrasher, and pondered whether he came over on the ferry, then lost his way in the storm. On the other hand, there was nowhere on the islet for him to stay. The farmhouse and the village of grass huts that formed part of the complex were the only inhabited buildings there.

She was glad to have taken an en suite bedroom in the house, given the storm. A few of the more hardy travellers had chosen to sleep in the huts, refusing to let the lashing rain deter them. In fact, they treated it all like an adventure. One woman, who had been to the islet for several years running, recalled sleeping soundly through much worse storms.

Outside the window the storm had abated slightly, and Shelley looked out towards the huts, some of which had lights on. Sixteen guests had opted to stay in them, and they each accommodated two people. The other four guests — Shelley, Mrs Caldicott, Miss Charters and Len — had taken rooms in the farmhouse.

It was a rule of the holiday that those choosing huts had to share with someone else. It surprised Shelley that, given everyone's earlier reticence, they agreed. So that meant, if she was right, that eight of the huts should be occupied. Yet she counted nine huts with lights on. The first eight were close together, nearest to the farmhouse, where they were afforded some shelter from the worst of the wind, whereas the last inhabited hut stood alone, down near the beach. It was probably the worst place to be, given the conditions.

She fancied she saw a figure approaching the hut, and then — almost as if the inhabitants of the hut knew she was observing them — the light flickered and went out.

Deciding she was starting to see intrigue where there was none, she tutted. It was just someone going to bed, that was all. Perhaps she had miscounted the guests, and there were twenty-one instead of twenty. Or perhaps it was one of the staff, who were probably not expected to share.

That led her to wonder if it were Paris, and she spent a pleasant five minutes imagining him lying in a truckle bed whilst the wind howled outside. He would be topless, of course, with his thick dark hair spread out on the pillow whilst he read a Booker Prize winner before turning the light out and going to sleep. She laughed at her own fancy. Most likely he was reading the latest Dan Brown, like most of the men on the plane coming over. And the truth was, she would probably like him better if that were the case. So, she imagined him lying there half-naked, reading Dan Brown and, she hoped, thinking about her. Then she remembered his quip about the face that launched a couple of jet-skis, and how he had looked at her when he said it, and decided he probably was not thinking of her.

Shelley's mother had always accused her of having an overactive imagination. That was why Tony had fooled her so easily, with his talk of lucrative deals. She assumed he had big ideas that needed a big canvas on which to paint them. Instead it turned his big ideas involved her money, costing Shelley the contents of her bank account, her house, which she had re-mortgaged at his behest, and very nearly her sanity. Tony had been prosecuted and imprisoned for fraud, but her money was lost forever. The stress of it all nearly caused her a nervous breakdown. Somehow she hung onto her sanity, but only just. She often felt that only a fine thread held it in place, and that one incident would snap it, leaving her catatonic.

At the age of thirty, she was back living with her mother and hating every minute of it. It was not just a step back in her life, but a step back in time, rendering her a child again, subject to the rules of a home that did not feel like her own any more. To make things worse, her mum liked to remind her about her stupidity on what felt to Shelley like a daily basis.

'Of course,' she would say, if Shelley complained, 'had you not been so sure that Tony was telling the truth — despite me warning you — then you'd still have your own house.'

Shelley sighed. Perhaps she was being too harsh. After all, her mum had not only taken her in when she needed it, but also paid for the holiday — though, as was the case with Len, Shelley suspected it had been more out of a desire to get her out of the way than from kindness.

'There you go again,' she said to herself, as she undressed. 'Imagining things that aren't necessarily so.'

Catching her reflection in the mirror, she saw a not unattractive young woman, with thick, dark auburn hair, and a pale face. Her almond-shaped green eyes were rimmed by the slightest trace of shadow; a testament to the many sleepless nights she had suffered over the past year.

She picked up her bag to find her mobile phone, supposing she ought to ring her mum and let her know she was safe. Assuming she could get a signal. That was the one thing she had not considered about the islet. Did it even have a transmitter?

When she reached into her bag, the contents felt strange. Like most women, she carried the same items with her all the time, along with a few old receipts when she had not bothered to clear out her bag for a while. But what she found was a thick wad of paper, which was definitely not meant to be there. Taking it out of her bag, she saw that it was a pile of yellowing letters, all addressed in German, to a Gretchen von Mueller.

She remembered Stefan's stumble, and how he had knocked her handbag to the ground. The only explanation was that he had hidden them in there. But why?

Opening one of the envelopes, she perused the letter within. Unsurprisingly they were all written in German. A language to which she had paid only scant attention in school. They were signed *Stefan*, but Shelley guessed it wasn't the man she'd spoken to, as the letters were dated early 1945. The man she met could have only been a child then.

Shelley took her laptop from her bag, hoping that she could get a satellite signal, despite the weather. It was intermittent, but she was able to get online, copying some of the text into an online translator. The pages took ages to load, and once or twice she lost the website completely. Finally, though, she was able to translate a good part of one of the letters, based on the words she could read and spell clearly.

Gretchen,

I hope that you and young Stefan are well. I am well, and . . . They say that we . . . I went . . . to Helena's bay, a pleasant part of the islet. It is quiet there, and I like . . .

My friend knows much about the history here, and told me . . . which are kept in a vault at the old church. Of course, I had to report this to my commanding officer, which made . . .

She does not understand duty as I do. She only worries about . . .

I must stop now as . . . Please . . . Stefan. I am missing so much of his childhood, but one day will return to you both and continue my duties as a father.

All my love,
Stefan

To Shelley the letter seemed strangely lacking in passion. She put it down to the Germanic mentality, but was still disappointed at the lack of romance. Especially all that stuff about duty. But she had probably watched too many war films, where everyone was so intense and living for the moment. In reality, for a young man stuck on a quiet Aegean islet, it probably all seemed a bit dull, and far away from the main action. There was no need to live for the moment. Or at least that's what Stefan von Mueller Senior must have thought at the time.

Whilst Shelley was online, she put the name Stefan von Mueller into a search engine and found a family site, run by what seemed to be an American cousin of the von Muellers, with pictures of an aristocratic young man in a soldier's uniform taken in the early 1940s, and marked Liuetenant Stefan von Mueller. Another picture showed Gretchen von Mueller and her son, a sturdy-looking German woman, with a young boy, whom Shelley presumed was the Stefan she met at dinner. At least it showed they existed, which gave Shelley some hope. The website asked for anyone who knew the family to contact Bertha von Mueller-Carter.

There was an email address, so she emailed the cousin, Bertha, and asked if she knew whether Stefan had indeed visited Agios Georgios Islet.

It was only as Shelley was closing the site down that she saw it had not been updated since the previous year. If she had not been so tired, she might have set about translating the rest of the letters. Instead, she put them away safely in her bag, and tried to settle down to sleep.

It was a struggle. She kept remembering the times she had pored over the Google Earth map of the islet before arriving. None of the three bays, as far as she remembered, was called Helena's Bay.

Sitting up in bed with her laptop resting on her legs, Shelley tried to get online again, but the satellite signal was down, probably due to atmospherics. She remembered seeing a map of the islet on the wall of the reception hall when they arrived.

She crept downstairs to find the front door ajar. So instead of looking at the map, she decided to wander down to the huts. She had no idea what she would do when she got there.

The storm had abated a little, but the wind and rain still battered Shelley as she made her way down to the hut. She had not thought to put on a coat, so very soon her clothes — jeans and a simple white vest top — were sticking to her skin.

Some of the huts still had lights on, and occasionally, despite the storm, she could hear the low hum of night-time conversation, as those who shared got to know each other. Perhaps, she thought, if she had bothered to share she would have someone to chat with, instead of feeling so out of the loop. She pushed the thought aside and walked down the sandy steps to the hut nearest the beach.

She hesitated. What could she do? Knock on the door? Disturb those inside? She crept nearer, hoping to hear someone talking. There was no sound at all, and the hut was in complete darkness.

Moving nearer, she was startled by the slamming of a door somewhere in the distance. Or was it thunder? She was not sure. The noise continued as if the door were off the latch.

'This was a good idea, Shelley,' she murmured. She remembered Annette's warning about not going out onto the islet on her own at night, and began to understand why it was good advice. If she shouted for help, chances are that no one in the far-off huts or the farmhouse would hear her over the storm.

Still her feet took her closer to the hut, determined to set her mind at rest. When she got there, she realised where the rattling noise came from. The door to the hut was off its latch, banging and clattering in the storm. She pushed it open, but it was empty. She was not surprised. No one could possibly sleep in there with the door banging open, letting in the elements.

Turning back towards the farmhouse, at much greater speed than that with which she had left it, she shivered, wishing she had put on a coat. She crashed through the open farmhouse door — and straight into Paris's arms.

'Shelley, what were you doing out in that weather?' he asked, his hands warm on her rain-chilled arms. She trembled, unsure that it had anything to do with her cold, wet state.

Standing so close, she could see just how smooth his tanned skin was, and smell the masculine aroma of the sea on his clothes.

'I . . . er . . . thought I left my book outside,' she said, her head bowed to hide the lie. This only served to bring her closer to his chest, which, she could see through the open neck, had a few fine dark hairs that spread upwards to his collarbone. She wondered if she could pretend to be disorientated for a moment longer, just to enjoy the sensation of being close to a man again. She reluctantly stepped back, gently disentangling herself from his arms.

'Surely it could have waited till the morning. Come on into the kitchen. I'll get you a towel and make you a hot drink.'

'No, I'm fine, honestly,' she said, looking down at the floor like a child caught doing something naughty. That was when she realised that her vest top had become almost transparent in the rain. To make matters worse, she noticed him noticing. Her subsequent blush covered not only her face, but also her neck and shoulders. At least it warmed her up a little.

'Perhaps you should go upstairs and get changed,' he said, grinning. 'But the offer of a warm drink is still there if you want it.'

'No, I've had enough excitement for

one night. Thanks very much for the offer, though.'

Feeling stupid, and very wet, she rushed up to her room where she showered and dressed for bed.

'It'll serve you right if you get ill,' she said to her reflection in the mirror, before climbing into bed and seeking warmth.

The room reminded her of the bed and breakfast places her parents used to take her to when she was a child. That was on the east coast of England, and more often than not there would be a storm. She used to snuggle down under the duvet, listening to the rain lashing against the window. Lying in the farmhouse, in a huge double bed, enwrapped in a thick blanket that she found in the wardrobe, she felt like a child again. All the worries of getting there, the storm outside, all the cares of the evening and her concerns about Stefan drifted away.

She idly thought about Stefan for a while, wondering where he was and if he was okay. But the last image in her mind, as she drifted off to sleep, was of Paris looking appreciatively at her in her wet clothes, enhancing the warmth she already felt.

3

In the morning she joined her group to help prepare breakfast. The previous evening, just before they'd gone to bed, Annette had split the guests into five groups of four people, and then gave them a rota.

'Your free time is your own,' Annette had told them, 'but we do encourage guests to be involved in the day-to-day domestic arrangements, including cooking, setting the table, washing dishes, laundry, helping out in the vegetable garden, and keeping the common areas tidy.'

'I didn't realise we'd paid to be used as skivvies,' Len had said.

'It is all part of the fun,' Annette said unconvincingly.

'And a good way for you all to get to know each other,' Paris had said, with rather more conviction.

Shelley was placed with Mrs Caldicott, Miss Charters and Len. She was poring over the map in the hallway when they came downstairs.

The weather outside was dull, but calmer, so some of the early risers were sitting at the tables on the terrace. As Brits, they were used to making the best of whatever weather was thrown at them.

'Time to get breakfast ready, Shelley,' Mrs Caldicott said. She appeared to have elected herself leader.

'I'm coming now.' Shelley smiled, and followed them to the kitchen. 'I was just looking at the map and trying to work out where Helena's Bay was. I can't seem to find it.'

'Is there a Helena's Bay?'

'I thought I heard someone say there was,' Shelley said vaguely.

'What's that?' Paris was waiting in the kitchen for them.

'Shelley was looking for Helena's Bay,' Miss Charters said. Her voice sounded odd. Guarded.

47

'There isn't a Helena's Bay on the islet,' Paris said, searching Shelley's face. There was something in his eyes that she could not quite fathom. 'It's so small that none of the bays have official names. Only those given to them by the locals when the islet was still inhabited. I've never heard anyone mention Helena's Bay.' She had the strong feeling he was withholding something. She opened her mouth to speak, but he talked over her, with what she thought was unnecessary abruptness. 'In the kitchen you'll find yoghurt, fruit and cereal. There's toast if anyone wants it, but ask first rather than waste bread, as we still can't get to the mainland. Come with me and I'll show you all where everything is.'

In the kitchen he pointed out the relevant cupboards, and the small utility room, which held the fridge and washing machine.

'Paris . . . ' Shelley hesitated, wondering how much she should say.

'Is this to do with your friend? What

was his name, Stefan?' Paris asked. He turned to her, with something like annoyance in his eyes.

She felt the heat of four pairs of eyes burning into her.

'I didn't imagine him,' Shelley said, folding her arms. 'In fact, he put some letters in my bag, so I can prove to you that he exists.'

'What letters?' Mrs Caldicott asked.

'They were in German. I managed to translate one online, but had no time to do the others. They were from his father to his mother, and mentioned visiting Helena's Bay. And I found a website for his family online. I've emailed his American cousin, Bertha, to ask if she knows where he is.'

'That's very interesting, dear,' Miss Charters said, 'but we really need to get breakfast ready. You can show us later.'

'I'm not imagining him,' Shelley said. She turned to Paris. 'I don't make up stories.'

'Perhaps we should talk about this after breakfast,' Paris said, his voice gentle. 'You can show me the letters, then we'll try and work out where Stefan went.'

'Don't bother humouring me.' Shelley grabbed up some cutlery and went out onto the veranda, slamming it down on the table.

For the rest of breakfast, she was quiet whilst everyone chattered around her. Then she remembered the huts.

'Someone was brave last night, sleeping in the hut nearest the beach,' she said, as lightly as she could. 'For a while at least. They seemed to have given up and come back to the farmhouse.'

The guests who had slept in them looked at her askance.

'I don't think any of us did,' a woman called Jean said. She was a hairdresser from Bradford. As such, her hair was a mixture of several different expertly applied colours and her make up immaculate, even at eight-thirty in the morning.

'Somebody did,' said Shelley. 'I saw a

50

light on in there. Perhaps it was one of the staff?'

Annette, Paris and a couple of the resident staff members looked up from their breakfast. 'All the staff sleep in the main house,' said Annette. 'Perhaps you imagined it.'

'Like the letters?'

'Letters?' Annette rested her chin on her hand, looking bored already.

'That Stefan left in my bag. About Helena's Bay.'

'There isn't a Helena's Bay, is there?' Annette turned to Paris, who shook his head.

Shelley couldn't miss the look everyone gave each other. She was clearly considered a complete fruitcake.

When everyone had gone back to eating breakfast, Mrs Caldicott leaned over to Shelley.

'I don't mean to be unkind, dear, but you're making everyone feel a little uncomfortable with all these questions. Why don't you let the matter of Stefan drop?'

Her kind warning might have been convincing if not for the fact that when Shelley nipped upstairs to get a jacket, she glanced out of her window and saw Mrs Caldicott going into the hut near the beach. A few minutes later, the old woman came out and gazed up towards Shelley's bedroom window. She began to wonder whether Mrs Caldicott had other reasons for stopping her asking questions.

* * *

The first morning's lesson was in making stained glass. It was presided over by a very elderly woman. Her long, blue-black hair was streaked with silver, and pulled up into a tightly wound knot on the top of her head. She wore a peasant-style dress and blouse, and sturdy black shoes.

'This is Yaya,' Paris told them when he led the guests to the workshop in some stables at the back of the farmhouse. At that time, Yaya was facing away from them, stooped down over her work. She turned and everyone gasped, and then tried to cover it by coughing. On the right side of her head was a big scar that started just below her hairline and spread across her temple. Yet her face was beautiful, showing evidence of once-perfect cheekbones and cornflower-blue eyes.

'Yaya was injured during the war,' Paris explained, reading everyone's minds. 'She lost her memory of that time.' He glanced across at Shelley, a look of warning in his eyes. 'Yaya still makes the most exquisite stained glass you've ever seen and she's going to teach you. Her English isn't very good, but she can explain herself well enough through hand signals. As far as making the stained glass is concerned, just watch her closely and copy her movements.'

'Couldn't you stay and translate?' Len asked. 'I mean, how are we supposed to learn if we can't understand a word she says?'

'You watch and pay attention,' Miss

Charters snapped. 'It's quite easy, even for a man.'

Shelley caught Paris's eye and they exchanged amused glances, the earlier tension forgotten for a moment.

'I'll see you later,' he said, looking straight at her.

It took the class a while to get used to Yaya's signals. She started by saying, 'Come, come,' and they had to join her around the main table, watching as she cut the glass into small pieces, then used glass paint to decorate it, before setting it in lead cames, using a small welding iron on the metal joints. The completed picture, just a few inches square but exquisite, was of a red rose.

'Now,' Yaya said. 'You . . . try.'

The next half hour was a mixture of precarious and hilarious, as fragments of glass flew into the air, landed on the floor, and at one point, in Jean's hair, getting caught up in her extensions.

'I'd send them a bill for that if I were you,' Len remarked.

Miss Charters tutted.

'They couldn't afford it,' Jean said. 'I had it done at the place where Posh Spice had hers done.'

'Is your salon not good enough, then?' asked Mrs Caldicott, her mouth twitching at the corners.

Despite the sparky discussion, Shelley could not help noticing that they all worked close together, whilst she worked alone at a table near to Yaya's. She had not intended to, unlike the evening before at dinner. It just worked out that way. Perhaps Mrs Caldicott was right. She was driving people away with her questions about Stefan.

'You . . . okay?' Yaya asked. It took a moment for Shelley to realise the old woman was addressing her.

'Yes, I'm fine,' Shelley said, nodding and putting a thumb up. 'Okay.'

'Cut,' Yaya said, pointing at Shelley's thumb. 'Blood.'

There was a hairline cut on the edge of the thumb, but it was bleeding quite heavily.

'Kitchen. Plaster,' Yaya said. They

were obviously words she had learned by heart for moments just like this.

'It'll be okay.' Shelley put her thumb into her mouth.

'No.' Yaya held up her hand, and pointed to a list of health and safety rules on the wall. 'Infection.'

'Oh, I see. Yes, all right. I'll be back soon.'

As she left, she felt the force of everyone staring at her, and wondered if she'd been labelled as the troublesome one. Or perhaps it was just her age, alienating her. She was at least twenty years younger than everyone else on the islet. Apart from Paris.

As if her thinking of him had conjured him up, he was in the kitchen when she got there.

'Is there a problem, Shelley?'

'Nothing serious. I cut my thumb and Yaya wouldn't let me continue until I'd put a plaster on it.'

'Let's take a look.' Paris reached up into a cupboard and pulled out a first aid kit. 'Come on, hold out your thumb.'

'I can dress it myself.'

'Okay, Miss Independent.' He handed her the box, and watched as she struggled to clean the cut and then wrap a plaster around her thumb one-handed. When the plaster folded in on itself and stuck solid before she had chance to put it on, she capitulated and held her thumb out.

Nothing prepared her for the bolt of electricity she felt when he touched her hand. It was all she could do to breathe as he tenderly wrapped the plaster around her thumb. Did she imagine it, or did he hold onto her hand for a little longer than necessary?

He smiled and turned away, busying himself with putting away the first aid kit. Shelley was about to walk away when he turned back to her and fixed her with a piercing gaze.

'Are you all right, Shelley? I sense you're not having a good time.'

'I'm fine,' she said. She was torn between wanting to show him the letters to prove her point, and hoping he would just forget the whole thing.

Every time she tried to explain, she ended up on the defensive, and it was an emotion she had experienced too many times, living back with her mother and trying to explain how she could be so stupid as to let Tony con her out of so much money. 'It's just, you know, being the youngest here and all that. I feel a bit out of it.'

'I hope you won't mind me saying this, but you should try to mix more.'

'I would if people weren't going out of their way to avoid me,' she answered sharply, pursing her lips.

'I'm sure they're not, Shelley. Sometimes we have to be the ones to make the effort. You know?'

'Thank you, I'll bear it in mind.'

'I've offended you.'

'No. You've just spoken the truth. I don't mix very well with other people. I used to, but . . . Anyway, thanks for putting the plaster on. I'd better get back to Yaya's class.'

'Don't worry about that. Why don't you show me Stefan's letters?'

'What? Now?'

'Seems as good a time as any.'

'Forget it. It doesn't matter. He's probably left the islet, now. Maybe they fell into my bag accidentally.'

'No one could have left the islet. The ferry isn't running again yet.'

'Couldn't someone have left by private boat?'

'There aren't any private boats. We'd like one, so we're no longer at mercy of the ferry company — as you know, they charge well over the odds — but at the moment we don't own one.'

'What happens if someone is sick and needs to leave the island?'

'We can get a rescue helicopter over from the mainland, but I can assure you that it hasn't visited recently. I don't understand, Shelley. You were eager to show me the letters earlier, to prove this man existed. Now you don't want to. Why?'

'All right, I'll show them to you. They're up in my room.'

Paris followed her up the stairs. When

they got to her door, it was standing slightly ajar.

'Someone has been in,' she said, pushing the door open gingerly.

'Are you sure you shut it?'

Shelley nodded. 'I locked it. I know I did.'

Everything in the room seemed to be in order, until she found her bag. It was where she left it, near the wardrobe, but she could tell it had been moved. Picking it up, she searched it for the letters.

'They're gone. Someone has taken them.'

'Really?' Paris was watching her closely, in a way she did not much like.

'They were in my bag. Look, I'll get my laptop and show you the website. I saved it on my favourites.'

But when she started up her laptop and opened up her Internet browser, the site was gone from the list. She checked the temporary Internet files and the history, but someone had wiped them clean, so that all trace of any webpages she had visited for the past goodness knows how many months had gone. She was notoriously bad at clearing the cache herself. Someone else must have done it. She tried the same steps again to find the website, using a search engine. Whilst there was a page listed on Google, when she clicked on the link there was just a plain white page with the message 'Error — Server Unavailable'.

'It was here,' she said, her cheeks feeling hot. Tears pricked her eyes, and she fought them back. There was no way she was going to cry in front of Paris, but it was all too much. 'There was a website, because I've found the link. So,' she said, trying to work things out in her head, 'whoever had that website has a reason for not wanting me to see it again. But what? Then there's the letters. How could they have gone?'

'Shelley,' Paris said. 'Sit down a moment.' He reached out to take her elbow, but she snatched her arm away and went to the window, staring out into the distance. She heard him sigh and out of the corner of her eye saw him sit down on the edge of the bed. Far in the distance she could see the jetty, where some men were waiting. There was someone on the seat near them, but she could not see who because they were blocking her view.

'I am not imagining it.'

'I know it's none of my business, but your mother contacted me. She was concerned about you, so told me a little of what's been going on. It sounds as though you've had a rough time of it.'

'So because a boyfriend conned me out of all my money I'm now making up stories about elderly German men?' She spun around. 'How did you jump to that conclusion?'

'I'm not jumping to conclusions. No one else saw him. You don't have the letters, and there's no website.'

'So you don't believe I saw him?'

'I believe that you believe it.'

'Oh, don't spout that psychological mumbo-jumbo at me. You still haven't explained why my experience with Tony . . . ' Her voice cracked slightly on her ex-boyfriend's name. 'How that would make me conjure up Nazi intrigue.'

'The history of this islet, and the Nazi occupation, is well-documented. Then you have a man who you say has returned to right the wrongs committed by his father. Maybe you associate what Tony did to you with what the Nazis did here. And you hope, deep down, that some-one will right the wrongs done to you.'

It was ludicrous, yet Paris made it sound so plausible that she could understand why he thought she was a total fruitcake.

'I don't think everyone is telling the truth about not having seen Stefan,' she said, as calmly as she could, whilst her tears threatened to betray her.

'Why would they lie, Shelley?'

'I don't know, but Mrs Caldicott warned me off talking about him, then a few minutes later she was snooping around the hut near the beach.'

'That is quite enough,' Paris said,

standing up. His blue eyes blazed with anger. 'I will not have you accusing the other guests here of being a part of this intrigue you've created.'

With that, he turned and stormed out of the room, leaving Shelley aghast. Obviously she had struck a nerve somewhere, but she did not know how. She turned back to the window, just in time to see the two men getting onto the ferry. The third man was between them, and he appeared to have trouble walking. His face hung down, making it difficult for her to see it clearly. Paris had told her that the sick were taken by helicopter, so why were they moving a man who seemed ill on the ferry?

Her first thought was of Stefan. They were getting him off the island without anyone knowing. She dashed downstairs and out of the door, running towards the jetty. It had taken them ten minutes to walk from there to the farmhouse the day before; it took her five minutes to run back, gasping as she did so. She was too late. By the time she reached the jetty the ferry was already on its way to the mainland.

She turned and ran back to the farmhouse, getting a stitch in her side in the process.

'I really need to go to the gym more,' she muttered to herself.

As she neared the office, she saw Paris coming out with Mrs Caldicott. They seemed to be having a heated conversation. Shelley forgot the niceties and rushed up to them.

'They took a man who's been hurt,' she gasped. 'On the ferry. You said they only used helicopters for the sick. I think it was Stefan.'

'Shelley . . . ' said Paris, a note of warning in his voice. He looked even angrier than before, but there was something else behind his eyes. Something that resembled fear.

Mrs Caldicott looked at them both, then turned to Paris.

'Just remember what I said.' With that, she walked off towards the terrace where Miss Charters was waiting.

4

'Are you going to tell me I imagined the two men carrying another man onto the ferry?' Shelley asked the next morning. She went to Paris's office as soon as she woke up, and found him with his head down over a pile of accounts.

The previous day had been strained, with Paris refusing to enter into any conversation about what Shelley had seen, other than saying, 'I'll look into it.' She spent another restless night, and when she finally woke, after two fitful hours' sleep, she began to wonder if she would have been better staying at home. She felt even more exhausted than when she arrived.

Even as she stood in front of Paris, asking her question, she found herself swaying with tiredness.

'No, the ferry pilot confirmed it. So did the two men who helped the man aboard. It was one of the archaeologists from the dig. He sprained his ankle, and rather than bother the helicopter rescue service, he insisted his friends take him over on the ferry.'

'They carried him like a sack of potatoes,' Shelley protested.

'His name is Professor Grunwald. He said you'd met. I've spoken to him on the phone this morning. He thanks you for your concern, but insists that his friends treated him quite well.'

'Grunwald? Yes, I met him.' Shelley's heart sank. She was desperate to be proved right about Stefan.

'Then you'll know he's about forty years old. That's not old enough to be a Nazi, is it?'

'You've obviously never heard of the BNP.'

'I grew up in Britain, and my mother is Jewish. You think I'd be ignorant of the British National Party?'

Greek father. Jewish mother. No wonder he had such exotic good looks.

'I'm sorry,' she murmured.

'What for? That my mother is Jewish?'

'No, of course not! I meant that I suggested you wouldn't have heard of the BNP. I was just being sarcastic anyway. I suppose . . . ' Her voice softened. 'It isn't very nice for you to hear me talking about Nazis and things, given what happened during the war. I don't want to cause anyone any anguish. I'll keep things to myself in future.'

'I'm not sure that's such a good idea. Anyway, all that was before I was born. I'm saddened and horrified, but I'm as detached from it as most people born after it was all over. Sometimes I think I should feel more, but it's hard when one is so disconnected from the actual time.' He paused, as if searching deep within himself. 'Are you satisfied that what I've told you about Grunwald is true?'

'I suppose I have to be,' Shelley said. In reality, she felt things were far from settled.

'Let it go, Shelley. Please.' Did she detect the hint of a warning?

'Of course.' She feared it would be obvious to him her smile was forced as it hurt her jaw to keep it in place. 'I'd better get to Yaya's class. It's pottery today, so hopefully I won't cut myself — unless I make myself dizzy with the wheel, or cause myself second-degree burns on the kiln.' She could hear herself twittering on and hated the sound. It was the same voice she used to her mother when she was lying to her about Tony's antics, because she was so sure he would put things right. 'I'll see you at lunchtime, yes?'

'Hmmm,' Paris replied. He did not seem convinced.

★　★　★

It was early evening before Shelley could get away from the others. When she first tried, after lunch, Miss Charters kept her talking with her reminiscences of holidays past.

69

'Then we went down the Nile,' she said, putting her hand on Shelley's arm, as Shelley tried to get up and leave the table. 'Have you ever been down the Nile?'

'No, and whilst I'd love to hear about it, I'm in a bit of a hurry,'

'We've plenty of time, dear. The afternoon class doesn't start for another hour. Where was I? Oh, yes, when you're out there on a steamer, the modern world seems to disappear. It was just like being in an Agatha Christie novel. Thankfully without the murder.'

When the afternoon class had finished around four, Shelley once again tried to escape, but was obliged to spend half an hour helping Mrs Caldicott find a missing phone charger.

'I was sure I packed it,' Mrs Caldicott said, turning her bag upside down and emptying the contents onto the table.

'Is it in your room?' Shelley asked, feeling that would be the most likely place.

'No, dear, I've looked there.'

'I know,' Shelley said, desperate to get away and convinced that Mrs Caldicott was trying to stop her. 'What sort of phone do you have? Mine might fit.' It occurred to Shelley as she said it that she had not charged her own mobile recently.

Mrs Caldicott held out her phone, but Shelley saw immediately that it was of a different make to hers.

'I don't know why they don't make them universal,' she said, shrugging. 'Oh, well, must be off.'

Shelley almost didn't get away at all. She reached the edge of the terrace, only to find Paris following her.

'Where are you going?' he asked. 'It's a bit late to go wandering off on your own, isn't it?'

She did some quick thinking, realising she'd never escape at this rate.

'I'm just off to the loo.'

'That's in the farmhouse. You're going towards the beach.'

'Yes, I thought I'd use the shower block near the top huts rather than traipse upstairs. That's all right, isn't it?'

'Yes, of course. Go ahead.'

Shelley guessed that he would not want to stand outside the ladies' waiting for her. She was also pleased to find that there were two entrances, so she entered by one, and left by the other, which brought her out at the far end of the huts, and only a few metres from the beach.

If what she had heard was correct, she could walk most of the way around the islet via the beach. At least she could get to where she wanted to go, which was the eastern bay where the archaeological dig was taking place. It took her half an hour to get there, and she began to realise that she may not get back until dark, which would make the beach harder to traverse. Especially if the tide came in.

Before she reached the bay, she left the beach, and climbed up onto the rocks above. For a moment she forgot why she was there, as she drank in the scenery. Over to the west, behind her, the sun was starting its slow descent into the sea, and far off, across to the east, she saw the faint lights of a distant coastline. She could not imagine a more perfect place. She looked around for someone to share that thought with, and was suddenly struck by her loneliness.

Miles away from home, and with people who either thought she was crazy or had suspicious reasons for pretending so, she felt adrift. Where was the comforting arm on her shoulder? Where was the deep, loving voice telling her the moment was more perfect because they shared it? Alarmingly, the voice she imagined belonged to Paris.

Shivering a little, she wrapped her pale blue scarf more tightly around her. An unbidden tear fell down her cheek. She brushed it away impatiently and walked further on, so she could have a good view of the bay. It was still light enough to see, and what she saw bothered her. Shelley was no expert on archaeology, but she knew from watching *Time Team* that archaeologists had to follow certain procedures. Part of that was returning the dig site to its original state afterwards. She saw no evidence of that procedure below. Only chaos. They were also meant to catalogue everything found, but she could see no workspace for that purpose.

The were also procedures regarding digging. It had to be done carefully, so that no artefacts found were damaged. But the group of men below her dug as if they were digging a grave; deep and violently, and without due care for the surroundings. At one point, a man stopped and picked up what appeared to be a piece of curved earthenware pot. He threw it aside and continued digging.

Shelley stepped forward to get a better view, at which point a rock dislodged and fell to the ground beneath her. Professor Grunwald looked up at her, fixing her with an intense stare.

Confused about her bearings, she started walking north, clutching her scarf around her. She heard him shout.

'Stop, Fraulein Freeman, please.'

Shelley did nothing of the sort. She kept on walking, slipping over the rocky ground once or twice. It took her several minutes to run to the northern end of the islet, convinced that they were following only a few metres behind her. It was stupid of her to come out alone, she realised that. There were no buildings or people on that side of the islet, apart from the so-called archaeologists working in the bay, and the farmhouse seemed a long way away, across the islet.

Finally, with her heart pounding in her chest, she stopped and looked down at a beach where a few bathers lay stretched out, enjoying what was left of the sinking sun. It was with some horror that she realised they were all completely naked.

She had stumbled upon the nudist beach that Annette mentioned. Her first instinct was to keep going along the coastline, but that would mean a lonely trip back to the farmhouse, and she was already exhausted from running. So she stumbled down on to the beach. She did not intend to join the bathers. Her intention was to make the men following believe that she had. She would sit it out near to the beach until she was sure the men had stopped following. As she grew nearer, she recognised Jean, the hairdresser, who was in very good shape, albeit somewhat overly cooked in the tanning department. Shelley dipped her head, not only hoping Jean would not see her, but also hoping she would not end up seeing old Len naked. It was more than her nerves could stand at that moment.

Not wanting to have to explain her presence, she kept to the edge of the beach. She looked back in the direction from which she came, and was sure she saw a man standing on the cliff overlooking the nudist beach. He ducked back out of sight so quickly that she wondered if it were just a trick of the light.

Walking along the beach, she prayed for the moment she could get out of sight behind some far off rocks. Out of the corner of her eye she could see someone coming out of the water. As the bather grew nearer, she became vaguely aware it was male. As he grew nearer still, passing the others and making his way to where she was, she realised it was Paris. She dared not look so kept her eyes fixed on some point above his head.

'Shelley! We wondered where you'd got to. What are you doing hiding up there? Don't be shy, come and join us.'

She shook her head, trying desperately to look anywhere but at Paris's naked body. The part she did see — his torso — was in very good shape, but it was as much as she dared to know about him.

'This was a bad idea,' she said, feeling hotter with every passing moment. She meant that going to the dig, and leaving herself open to being chased by the men, was a bad idea, but Paris didn't take it that way and she was not about to share the whole experience with him.

'Oh, come on. Being nude isn't obligatory.'

She shook her head vehemently, and in the process saw that he was wearing a pair of black swim shorts. His body was firm and toned, with fine hair tracing from his navel, down under the waist band of the shorts. A deep blush started from her toes, all the way up to the roots of her hair. There was no way she could relax with a half-naked Paris nearby.

'I'm on my way back to the farmhouse,' she said. 'I need to be alone for a while.'

'Are you all right? You look upset.'

Should she tell him? She looked back towards the rocks, but could see none of the men who had been following her. What if they were lying in wait?

'I'd like to go back, but I wondered . . .'

'Yes?'

'Whether you'd mind walking back with me. Just for company.'

'I'd be delighted to.' His face spread into a smile. 'Actually, it's time everyone were getting back for dinner. I'll tell them.'

Shelley struggled to suppress a crushing sense of disappointment.

5

'Do you live here all the time?' Shelley asked as they made their way back to the farmhouse. Jean and the others walked about fifty yards behind, so to all intents and purposes Shelley and Paris were alone. It was almost dark. In the distance the farmhouse lights twinkled, adding a welcoming glow to the cool night air.

'No, only during the summer. The dream is that one day we can offer all year round breaks, but until the centre pays its own way, I have to go back to England to work in the winter.'

'What do you do?'

'I'm a counsellor.'

'Of course you are.' She grinned. 'It was obvious, really. The way I feel as if you're reading my mind.'

Paris laughed.

'It always unnerves people. I should

learn to switch off more.'

'Is it because of your counselling work that you had the idea of offering holistic breaks?'

'Sort of. I spend a lot of time working with people who lack direction. The idea is that trying lots of different activities here might set them on the right path. It may not be anything we actually do here. Being here sometimes just helps people to decide what they *don't* want out of life.

'So what do you do in the real world, Shelley? I know you work in a law centre, but in what capacity?'

'Do you mean to say my mother didn't tell you every detail of my life?'

'No, she didn't. She only told me what happened with Tony.'

'I represent people in employment tribunals. Discrimination, non-payment of wages. That sort of thing.'

'Do you like your work?'

'It's like any job. It can be very rewarding one minute and have me tearing my hair out the next. We're overworked, underpaid and under-staffed, like most charities, so I work really long hours. Employment laws are all very well, but if there's work to be done, and people are relying on you, you sometimes have to work beyond what's legal to help those who have no choice. I think that's why . . . '

'Why what?'

'Nothing.' She had been going to say that was why Tony had managed to con her. They'd met just after she had finished a very difficult case. She was exhausted from not leaving the office till eight o'clock most evenings. So when Tony paid attention to her in the pub, she was ripe for a distraction. But she feared Paris would not allow her that excuse. Because it was one that, as an intelligent woman, she barely allowed herself.

'You wonder how, with your experience, you could be taken in by a con man,' Paris said.

'You're doing it again. Unnerving me.' There were many more reasons for

81

her feeling unnerved in his presence than him reading her mind. He had not bothered to dress for the walk back, carrying his clothes over his arm. His very nearness was enough to throw her emotions off kilter. And that terrified her. After Tony, she vowed never to trust another man. She would never let anyone get close to her and make her vulnerable again.

Not that she believed Paris was interested in her in anything other than a professional capacity. At best, she brought out his caring side. At worst, she was an interesting case study, and the Stefan stuff had only served to make her more interesting.

'I'm just trying to tell you to stop being so hard on yourself, Shelley. People make mistakes. We trust others because we're basically honest human beings ourselves and we've a tendency to believe the best of people. When you love someone, it's harder still to believe the worst in them, as you think it reflects on your judgment. But when they let you down, it's their failure. Not yours.'

'A year ago, I had a home of my own and money in the bank. Now, at the age of thirty, I'm back living with my mother and if she hadn't paid for this holiday I wouldn't be here. How can I not feel a failure, Paris?'

He stopped and turned to her, putting his hand on her shoulder. She liked the way it felt.

'Because you're not. A lot of people would want to hide under the duvet and never leave the house again. I've seen it happen during my work in supporting victims. But despite your misgivings about being here, you came. That's because, deep down, you haven't given up. You're getting your life back on track. The fact that your mum had to pay is of no importance. Allowing that took some courage, too. She loves you a lot, you know.'

'Really? She's the one who keeps telling me I'm a failure.' Shelley walked on, not wanting to push Paris away, but feeling even more unsettled by his touch. She told herself he only meant to be kind, yet she couldn't ignore the electricity that passed from his fingers through the fabric of her T-shirt.

'Does she? I got the impression your mum thinks she's the one who's failed, because she couldn't make you see that Tony was a conman. She blames herself for not trying harder to make you see the truth.'

'You got all that from my mother?' It seemed unlikely to Shelley. Her mum was as tough as they came.

'Reading between the lines, yes.'

'Hmmm! My mum doesn't have anything between the lines. She's a completely open book. What you see is what you get.'

'No — the way I see it, you feel defensive about what happened, so you've read your mum wrong.'

'Thank you, Sigmund.'

'For the record, I hate Freud.'

They walked the rest of the way in silence, but not the uncomfortable kind. She felt safe with him there. She might tease him about his tendency to analyse people too much, but a lot of what he said she knew deep down to be the truth.

'Tell you what,' Paris said as they neared the farmhouse. 'I've got to go to the mainland tomorrow to pick up some supplies. Why don't you come with me? We'll get away from the wrinklies for a bit. We could have a couple of hours over there, and maybe get some lunch. I could show you around the town, too.'

There had been no one in her life since Tony. She'd not been short of offers for dates, but she'd turned them all down. The idea of spending time alone with Paris was more appealing than Shelley could have imagined. Nevertheless, she was surprised to hear herself reply with more enthusiasm than she intended.

'Oh, yes, that would be lovely.'

'I think so, too,' Paris said gently.

Shelley did not know how she made

it through the next morning. The lesson was Dancing with Silk, and involved them twirling around the room, waving large silk ribbons after them. At first they all felt a bit daft, but that gradually turned to laughter. Especially when Len threw himself into it with such aplomb, like a latter-day Rudolph Nureyev. Shelley wondered what his friends at the police social club he often spoke of would think of him. Her guess was that if they were here, he would not enjoy himself nearly as much.

She realised that was the point of this holiday. To take people out of themselves. Have them doing things they wouldn't normally do. And if it all felt a bit silly, what did it matter? Yaya was laughing, too, clapping her hands to the music to show that she certainly didn't expect everyone to take it all too seriously.

Paris came to get her just before noon, and stood laughing because she had somehow got herself tied up in Mrs Caldicott's ribbons as well as her own.

As she giggled, struggling to break free, he watched her with what looked like appreciation in his eyes.

'Oh, hang on, dear,' Mrs Caldicott said, 'I think that's your ribbon. No, no, it's mine. This one is yours. No, that one's mine, too. Oh, no, it isn't. It's Minnie's. Minnie, dear, it would have been much better had you not attempted to free us. Now we're all tied up.'

Shelley realised that, for the first time in a long time, she was really laughing, right down to the pit of her belly. Tears rolled down her cheeks as they became more and more entangled, until Yaya, also laughing, came along and deftly sorted out the ribbons.

Finally Shelley was able to free herself and join Paris.

'You looked very pretty, wrapped up in all those colours,' he said as they walked amiably to the jetty. She was glad that her face was already flushed from dancing, so he could not see her blush. 'Not that you don't look lovely in that dress.'

She had agonised over what to wear, and settled on a plain white shift dress, which had a black band around the waist. She had brought it in case dinner turned out to be a formal affair.

'Very Audrey Hepburn,' Paris said.

'Oh, in that case, I'd better put on my huge sunglasses,' Shelley replied, taking them out of her handbag and putting them on. 'There, does that complete the image?' She tried to sound flippant, not wanting to let on how nice it was to be compared to someone who was still considered one of the most beautiful women ever to have lived. In her heart, Shelley knew that she was neither as beautiful or as slender as Audrey, but walking along a beach road, with a handsome man at her side, she allowed herself the fantasy of pretending to be just for that day.

Paris stood back, and put his hands in the formation of a frame, squinting through it with one eye.

'Absolutely perfect, dahling,' he said, affecting a Cary Grant accent. 'Now, let's go and have *Breakfast At Tiffanys*. Well, I don't think we'll get that far in one afternoon. Let's just make it lunch at a nice little taverna I know near the church.' He held out his arm, in a gallant gesture, and she threaded her own arm through it.

As they walked the last few steps to the jetty, Shelley hoped that he was not standing close enough to her to feel her heart beating rapidly. His arm on hers felt safe and strong, and as both their arms were bare, there was also the delicious sensation of skin on skin, sending a thrill through her whole body.

She felt both excited and confused at the same time. Did he like her as much as she liked him? Or was he just being nice to her, either because he thought she was a bit unstable or because she was the only person near his age on the islet? As kind as he was to the older guests, she reasoned it must be nice for him to spend time with people of his own age occasionally.

Or, she thought more darkly, maybe

he made a point of singling out one woman every week for his attentions? Her brother, Rob, had once worked as an entertainer in a holiday camp, and was always coming home with tales of his conquests. That was before he met his wife, and fell hook, line and sinker into marriage and two point four children. But it had taken him a very long time to get there.

Shelley decided it was best just to enjoy the day and not seek too much from it. That way she would not get her heart broken again. As that thought entered her head, it also occurred to her that Paris might have the ability to hurt her more than Tony ever had. When she finally accepted that Tony was conning her, she was not heartbroken in the sense of being madly in love with him. Thinking about it, she did not know if she had ever really been that much in love. Or maybe she just told herself that to lessen the pain? No; she had been infatuated, but not in love. She had always known that they would not spend their lives together. Part of her was relieved that it was finally out in the open and she had to deal with it head-on. She was more hurt by the way he had left her — broke and humiliated, living off her mother's charity.

The ferry ride to the mainland was a far more sedate affair than their stormy arrival several days earlier. The Aegean Sea twinkled in the sunlight. Shelley rested against the railings, looking out. She was glad that Paris was not the sort of man who demanded conversation all the time. He just stood next to her, their bodies not quite touching, but close enough for her to feel the warmth of his. It made her feel, at least for that moment, that she could trust him with anything.

'What you said about my mum,' she said, after a long, comfortable silence. 'I think you're right. I've been too hard on her. You see . . . my dad did the same thing to her. Not quite as spectacularly as Tony did with me, but when he died he left Mum with thousands of pounds worth of debt. It was lucky that the house we lived in was rented, otherwise we'd have been homeless. But because he'd talked her into having so much of the debt in her name, it took her years of hard work to pay it off. I think she's disappointed in me because she thought I'd learn from her mistake.'

'I don't think she's disappointed in you at all, Shelley. How could she be? You're a bright, charming young woman who does good work helping others. She's probably just sad that she wasn't able to save you from making the same mistake. Parents don't realise that sometimes they have to let their kids make their own mistakes. It's the only way any of us learn.' His blue eyes darkened considerably and he gazed out into the sea, as if he saw something there that caused him immense pain.

'You sound as if you're speaking from bitter experience,' she said, tentatively, reluctant to pry too much.

Paris took a deep breath and

clenched his jaw, as if fortifying himself against what was to come.

'When I was younger, I got in with a bad crowd. Did some really stupid things. Drink, wild parties, casual affairs. My mum and dad tried to warn me, but I wouldn't listen to anyone, let alone them. Then, when I was twenty-two, one of my friends, Harry, was driving while heavily drunk. He killed a woman crossing the road and died from his own injuries a few days later.

'When I saw his parents at his funeral, I witnessed their guilt and shame that the son they'd invested so much time in not only killed himself, but also took someone else with him. Harry was a good person underneath all that wildness, but that's not how people remember him. Who can blame them when an innocent life is lost? It could have so easily been me, driving that car in that state. I knew then that I never wanted to put that same pain and shame on my parents' faces. I cleaned up my act, and decided I wanted to help victims come to terms with their loss.'

'I'm so sorry for your friend and for the woman who died,' Shelley said, putting her hand on his arm. She admired his frankness about his earlier life, and was slowly but surely beginning to think of him as Mr Wonderful.

★   ★   ★

Paris only had to pick up a few supplies, mainly for the office. He arranged for them to be left at the jetty before the last ferry left at five o'clock, then he and Shelley walked around the small town. After a delicious lunch in a quiet taverna, where they chatted happily about art, music, books and films, they found themselves at the church.

It was cool inside, just as it had been on the day they arrived, but this time there was no impending storm. Once again, Shelley was enthralled by the play of light on the stone floor. It was almost, but not quite, as beautiful as the windows themselves.

'Annette said that Yaya maintains these windows,' Shelley said as she and Paris sat close together in a pew. She was not sure she should be feeling the things she felt, so she waffled on, hoping to distract herself from his proximity. 'She does it beautifully. Much better than my sorry effort the other day in the stained glass class.'

'It's the one thing of which she's very proud,' Paris said. 'She refuses to let anyone else near them, despite many offers of help. The trouble is — ' He paused a moment, his face becoming sad. 'She won't be with us forever, and there aren't many left now who have her skills. I've tried to persuade her to teach others, but she won't be budged.'

'I can't blame her for feeling a bit possessive,' Shelley said. 'But you're right, it would be sad if there were no one left to care for them. I hope you don't mind me asking, but is sitting in a Christian church an ambivalent feeling for you? I mean, with your mum being Jewish.'

'I always feel I'm lucky to have my feet in both cultures,' he said. 'And extra fortunate to have parents for whom religion doesn't really matter. What matters is how good a person is inside, not which gods or saints they choose to worship.'

Shelley nodded her agreement. Her mum had brought her up to believe the same.

'Does your mum ever come here? I mean, to the islet?' Shelley asked.

For some reason Paris changed the subject completely.

'I forgot. There's a museum in the town, and in there is a picture of Yaya as a young woman, taken just after the war. Would you like to see it?'

'Yes, that would be very interesting.'

He led her to a small but steep side street. Part way up the hill was a tiny entrance into an even tinier museum. Most of the artefacts inside were either from the classical period of Greek history, or from the second World War.

'This house was where the Resistance

used to meet,' Paris explained, 'so it seemed the obvious place for the museum. It's small, but holds a lot of history in its tiny walls.'

'My grandfather used to collect World War Two memorabilia,' Shelley told him as they started to look around. 'It was a passion of his.'

'Was?' Paris looked sympathetic.

'He's not dead,' she explained. 'But sadly, he had to sell a lot to pay his care home fees. He just kept a few old medals. It would be nice to think that some of the stuff turned up in museums, but I doubt it.'

'That is a pity. More people should be able to see them. It brings the whole experience to life when you can see the artefacts. The Aegean Islands were occupied by the Germans right up until 1945,' he said, explaining the exhibits as they walked around. There were old landmines and shell casings, alongside documents from that time. 'But the mainland was free from occupation several months earlier, in 1944. It is said

97

that the entire Jewish population of Greece was wiped out.' He stopped for a moment, and Shelley felt it wise to say nothing. There were some horrors for which there were no suitable words. 'The Greeks didn't fare much better. The Nazis murdered entire villages. Can you believe that? Whole families wiped out in the blink of an SS officer's eye. They looted quite a lot, too. I don't know if anyone's told you, but they stole the rubies from the church on the islet. No one has ever been able to find them.'

They moved further into the museum, which was dark apart from the lights illuminating the exhibits. The space was so small they spent much of the time standing extremely close together.

'Here, this is Yaya,' Paris said. It was a picture of a very beautiful young woman standing outside the local hospital. Shelley was surprised to see that she was heavily pregnant. 'See,' he pointed to a printed card beneath the picture, 'there's her name. Helena Georgiadis.'

Shelley froze, but Paris did not seem to notice. He moved on, then realised she had stopped. She stared up at him.

'Oh, I'm sorry,' he said. 'This was a stupid idea. Fancy bringing you to this miserable place on what's supposed to be our lovely day out.'

'No, no,' Shelley said, struggling to regain composure. 'It's fine. I just felt a shiver run up my spine, that's all. All that sadness . . . ' Her voice faded away, and she hoped that the explanation for her sudden change satisfied him. It seemed to. He took her by the arm, and led her back to the ferry.

She was quiet on the crossing back to the islet, but thankfully he was, too, both lost in contemplation. But she did not want to be silent. She wanted to ask him why when she had mentioned Helena's Bay, he had not thought to mention that Yaya's first name was Helena.

It was the sort of thing that most people would do, she reasoned to herself, and she could almost hear him say it aloud, *No, there's no Helena's Bay but that's Yaya's name*. But the trip across was a long one. By the time they reached the islet, and he had chatted to her a little more, she had convinced herself she was being silly.

After all, she could have found out Yaya's name herself, had she but asked. In fact, it was probably on the holiday brochure, amongst the listed classes. Paris may have even assumed she knew it because of that, which meant he had no need to remind her when she mentioned it. She realised she would probably look really foolish if she brought it up and that were the case. Another instance of her supposed delusions. And it had been such a wonderful day, apart from that one moment of awkwardness at the museum. She wanted the blissful feeling to last.

So when he held out his hand once the ferry had pulled in, she took it gladly, and they walked hand in hand to the farmhouse together.

6

Dinner was a much more relaxed affair than the previous evenings, with wine and good conversation flowing freely. Shelley laughed more than she had for a long time as Len treated them to tales of the hapless criminals he had arrested over the years, and Miss Charters talked of her own time as a dancer at the Windmill Club.

It was hard for Shelley to believe that the demure Miss Charters was once in a nude review.

'It was much more modest than it sounds,' Miss Charters told the diners. 'Everything was in those days. We weren't allowed to move in case anything jiggled. That was until someone let a mouse loose on the stage. Then everything jiggled. I received at least five proposals of marriage after that night. Turned them all down, fool that I am.'

After dinner, someone put music on, and Yaya taught them Greek dancing. She explained, translated by Paris, that the island dances were 'Watery' in flow and tone, and showed them how to perform them.

Once the British guests got over their initial reserve, they all began to enjoy themselves, whilst Len did his impression of Zorba the Greek, dancing out of time with all the others but not caring at all.

Shelley felt a hand in hers, and saw Paris standing next to her, whilst Mrs Caldicott took her other hand. There was something secure about the way they held on to her, though she was honest enough to admit that it was Paris's hand which made her feel the safest. With wine filling her veins and a newfound sense of peace, she allowed the dance to carry her away from all the cares of the past year. Tony was forgotten. Her mother was forgotten. Stefan was forgotten. The sinister men on the east bay were forgotten. After all, how could anything be sinister on this wonderful islet? All she felt was the music and Paris's strong hand holding hers.

She decided that despite their little idiosyncrasies, these were good people. Mrs Caldicott might be a bit stern, but she was kind to everyone, ensuring they all had plenty of food and drink, clucking like a mother hen over those who seemed a bit lonely, insisting they join in the fun. Len might moan a bit but he was a good laugh when he let go and forgot he was supposed to be a sensible ex-policeman. Miss Charters, though a bit bird-brained at times, was a sweetie with lots of funny tales to tell. Even June, with her brittle salon-manager manner, turned out to be good company. Shelley wondered then if that was what the holiday was all about. Cracking through the tough shell people built around themselves in the outside world.

The air was heavy with the scent of jasmine and the ozone from the sea. If

Shelley were asked to describe paradise, this would be it. Miles away from the hustle and bustle, with no exhaust fumes or roaring engines. Only the soft hush of the sea as it touched the shore, and the occasional cicada chirping out a night song. And Paris's hand in hers, adding to the romance of it all. It felt like a night when good things could happen — and she'd had precious few of those in the past few years.

They had begun on the terrace, but gradually the line of dancers snaked down to the beach, where soft sand slipped between their toes. Even when they were too far away to hear the music clearly they danced. Some broke off and ran into the water.

Suddenly Shelley felt herself pulled in that direction, and Paris dragged her into the waves. There was something exhilarating about getting her clothes soaking wet. It felt boisterous and daring. Even more so than if she were naked. Her dress clung to her trim figure, whilst her red hair, usually flattened with straighteners, curled around her temples.

'Aphrodite, I presume,' Paris said softly. They had moved away from the others, and were standing alone some way along the coast. The water helped cool the fever she felt at being close to him.

She smiled shyly at the compliment, admiring how his own clothes clung to his lean frame.

'Don't tell me,' she teased. 'I've got a face that could launch a couple of jet skis. Oh, no, that was the Helen to whom you aspire.'

'Actually when I said that and then looked at you, I was wondering if a thousand ships would be nearly enough.'

Glad that it was dark, so that once again he could not see her blush like a silly schoolgirl, she smiled and turned to look up towards the farmhouse, where the lights on the terrace twinkled comfortingly.

'That's a kind thing to say. Thank you.'

A moment later she felt his hand on her shoulder. He turned her gently back to face him and put his hand beneath her chin, raising her face to his. The world seemed to stand still as his lips found hers for a tender kiss. Lacing her arms around his neck, she allowed herself to enjoy the moment. The kiss became deeper, more passionate, and his hands splayed out on her back, as if he wanted to touch as much of her as possible. She was not averse to the idea herself, feeling his chest and the beating of his heart through his wet shirt.

She pulled away reluctantly.

'Is this allowed? You know, is it ethical and all that?'

'I'm not your counsellor, Shelley, despite you insisting on believing so.'

'In that case,' she said, putting her arms back around his neck, 'I'd quite like another kiss, please.'

Their second kiss was much deeper, and more passionate. Shelley had no idea how much time passed, whether it was moments or millennia. They could just as well have been lovers from ancient Greece, or lovers from the future — and like all lovers, they created their own time.

After a long time holding onto each other, they took a leisurely walk back to the farmhouse. The others gave them knowing smiles and winks as they approached the terrace.

'I . . . er . . . think I'll go and phone my mum,' Shelley said. There was no hiding her blushes that time. The lights on the terrace revealed all. 'I'll see you soon,' she said to Paris, hoping he would understand the invitation, then worrying that she might be offering it too soon. She was not a girl of easy virtue, preferring to be in love before she slept with any man. But, as one of her favourite songs went, *if this was not love, why did it feel so good?*

⋆　⋆　⋆

After her chat with Paris, she was feeling a bit guilty about how she had

107

treated her mum, Pat, since the problems with Tony. Pat had wanted to help her, but Shelley had pushed her away, feeling she was being judged all the time. Yet her mum had been there for her, giving her a home and money when she needed it. All she had given in return were bad moods and silence.

She rushed upstairs to get her mobile phone. She hoped there would be a signal now that the storm had passed. But that was the least of her problems. The battery was flat and she could not find her charger. Which was odd; she remembered putting it in her case. Mrs Caldicott had said something about losing her phone charger, too, had she not?

Shelley shook her head. 'Don't start seeing reds under the bed again, dear,' she muttered, in a good imitation of Mrs Caldicott's stern tones. Wondering if Paris might let her use the office phone, she nipped back downstairs.

As she drew nearer to his office, she heard voices from within. She was about to walk away when she heard a man say in an accent direct from the north of England, 'You must keep that lass away. She's threatening to ruin everything we're working for. We are so close to finding the rubies.'

Shelley gasped. *That's* what they were looking for at the bay.

The other voice was indistinct, no more than a murmur. But it sounded soothing, as if trying to placate the man.

'Yeah, I know you say no one believes her, but they might if she keeps on. Someone's already contacted the mainland, asking about the old bloke.'

Shelley moved closer to the door, then realised that the voice was coming nearer. She ducked back out of the way and hid in a small sitting room across the hall, peering through the crack in the door. She saw the man from the beach leave the office. It was Professor Grunwald.

For a horrible moment, she thought he had seen her. She drew further into the room, until she heard him leave via the back door. She watched from the window as he walked towards the huts, and down onto the beach, presumably intending to take the same route she had. It was interesting to note that, for a man who had supposedly hurt his ankle, he did not limp.

She watched him for a while until he faded out of view, and then went back to the hall. When she got there, the office door was open and Paris stood framed by it, looking quizzically back at her.

'Is everything alright, Shelley? You look pale,' he said.

Struggling to remain composed, Shelley smiled. In reality she wanted to burst into tears, but she would never be weak for a man again. All that rubbish he had said about her not feeling guilty. All that pretended understanding about her mother. The day on the mainland. The kissing. All he had been doing was keeping her sweet, whilst he and his friends got on with their illegal pursuits

— and, worse, hurting a harmless old man. Within seconds she convinced herself the only reason he took her to the mainland was to get her out of the way whilst they did something else illegal.

'Yes, I'm fine. Just a bit of a headache from the sun. I think I'll have an early night.'

'Would you like company?' he asked, a note of suggestion in his voice.

'No.' It came out more sharply than she intended. 'I mean — no, sorry. I'd really like to be alone for a while.' She turned towards the stairs and climbed two steps.

'Shelley?' His voice was smooth, and made the hairs on the back of her neck tingle. Oh, how she hated him for being so attractive. But, from her recollection of films, bad guys always were.

'Yes.' She half turned to look down at him. Even with her standing a couple of steps up, he was taller than her. Instinctively she climbed a couple more, to gain the upper hand.

'I'd like to know what's brought the shutters down again.'

'I don't know what you mean.'

'I thought you and I had made some headway today. You opened up to me, as if you were starting to trust me. Didn't our kisses mean anything?'

Opening her mouth to speak, Shelley found she had nothing to say that would not set her off in floods of tears. Swallowing back a lump in her throat, she managed a response.

'You've certainly said all the right things.'

'What's that supposed to mean?'

'Oh, Paris, it doesn't mean anything. Sometimes a cigar is just a cigar, all right!' She turned and ran up the stairs, as the tears began to flow freely down her cheeks.

When she got to her room, she threw herself on the bed, crying. But soon she steeled herself, and sat up, impatiently rubbing the tears from her face. She would not cry over another conman. He had been so nice to her. Perhaps it was easy for him because she wanted to believe that there was one nice man in the world.

Thinking back, she remembered him saying that he could not afford to stay on the islet all year round, but he wanted to. Was that why he and his friends were searching for the rubies? So he could have the money to run the centre all year? And if so, did the means justify the ends?

Shelley decided it did not. The rubies belonged to the church. What's more, people had died on this islet and throughout the Greek mainland. All over Europe, in fact. The rubies were quite rightly red, to denote the blood shed so that they and other treasures like them could be sold from the innocent people who owned them.

Yet she wanted to give Paris that excuse. That he only wanted the money so he could run the centre and give people wonderful holidays. But after all he had said in the museum, about those who died, sounding sympathetic as he did, she could not allow it. Would not allow it. That was the mistake she made with Tony. Allowed him excuse after excuse.

Some things were inexcusable, no matter how much in love with a person you were. And foolishly, stupidly, infuriatingly, she realised, as the tears began to flow again, she had allowed herself to fall for another conman.

7

The following morning, after a bad night's sleep, she vowed to avoid Paris. That was not too difficult. When she arrived at breakfast, he left, his face a mask of some emotion she could not fathom. She also had to avoid being kept from going about her own pursuits by Mrs Caldicott and Miss Charters. After a singing class, where Len and June regaled everyone with their version of *I Got You Babe*, Shelley decided to go investigate what was going on.

Despite their best efforts and an infusion of guilt which Shelley's mother could have learned from, she politely declined to help Mrs Caldicott find a missing scarf or assist Miss Charters with her attempts to finish a jigsaw.

'Are you sure, dear? It's most relaxing, you know, and you seem a bit stressed,' Miss Charters said, holding up a piece of blue sky that looked like a hundred other pieces of blue sky on the table.

It struck Shelley that the jigsaw was a bit like the islet. Everyone fitted together in some way. She just needed to work out how.

The previous evening she had felt warmth for these people, even something approaching affection. Now, because she did not know who to trust, they irritated her. But she was a good enough person to feel bad about that, because Mrs Caldicott and Miss Charters had only ever been kind to her — albeit in a schoolmarmish type of way.

'I'm sorry,' she said, not sure if she could stop herself from crying, 'I'd really like some time alone.'

'Very well, dear,' Mrs Caldicott said, her voice softening. 'We don't want to crowd you. But if you do ever need someone to talk to, we may be a couple of chatty old birds, but we have seen a lot of the world.' The older woman looked in the direction Paris had gone. 'There's nothing that can't be mended after a nice chat and a cup of tea.'

'I'm afraid that's probably not true,' Shelley murmured, making her escape before the tears fell again.

Her first stop was the jetty. The singing class had ended about half an hour before the ferry arrived, which gave her plenty of time to get into place. It was only as it sailed into view and she saw the rugged Greek pilot that she realised he may not know a word of English. It also occurred to her that he might well be in on whatever was going on.

By the time the small boat pulled up to the jetty, Shelley had more or less convinced herself that the idea was a stupid one. She turned to go back to the farmhouse, and saw Annette coming along the path towards her.

'Are you off to the mainland again, Shelley?'

'No, actually, I just wanted to speak to the ferryman — only it's occurred to me that he may not speak English.'

'He doesn't, but I can translate if you want me to.'

'No, it's fine, honestly,' Shelley said. 'It was a silly idea anyway.'

'No, come on, let me help. Are you trying to book a trip?' Before Shelley could answer, Annette had whistled to the ferryman to come ashore.

He landed on the jetty with a thump that very nearly broke through the old planks. Annette looked at Shelley, expectantly.

'I wanted to ask him if he brought an old German man here on Saturday,' Shelley said, wishing she had not started this.

Annette, showing no surprise at Shelley's question, turned to the ferryman and translated.

'No, he wasn't on duty that day. I think his son was in charge of the ferry that day.'

'The other day,' Shelley said. 'When a man was taken to the mainland with his sprained ankle. Was this ferryman on duty?'

It turned out he had been.

'Ask him,' Shelley said, feeling her

cheeks grow hot. 'If that was an old or young man.'

Annette and the ferryman exchanged words for quite a while, with lots of hand waving and gesticulating. Annette turned to Shelley.

'He was neither young nor old. He was about forty.'

'Oh.' Shelley was perplexed. She felt sure the conversation had been longer than that. Then again, she knew no Greek, so chances are it took a lot of words to ask a question that might only take a few words in English.

Annette had a few more words with the ferryman, explaining to Shelley that Paris had ordered some jet skis.

'He's trying to encourage more young people to the islet,' she explained, sounding less impressed than she ought to be.

'It was Professor Grunwald. You know that, don't you?' Annette said when the ferryman returned to his boat and they were walking back towards the farmhouse.

'Yes, of course,' Shelley said. 'I just

wondered if it might have been someone else.'

'The man you saw on the first night?'

'Yes, that's right.'

'We haven't seen him on the islet at all, and there's no way that he could have left.'

'Are you going to tell me I'm still imagining it?' Shelley retorted. 'And did I also imagine that when Professor Grunwald visited Paris last night he spoke with an English accent?'

'No! Are you sure?' Annette asked.

'Yes, I know a Yorkshire accent when I hear one.'

'Well, that's amazing. I mean, he speaks English — but always with a German accent. Mind you, I always thought there was something a bit fake about him.'

'That's not all,' Shelley said, finding that once she started speaking, everything that had bothered her poured out. Annette turned out to be a good listener. 'He hasn't got a limp, which you'd think he would have. And the dig isn't right somehow. They're digging like navvies. I'm not an expert, but I thought archaeological digs were supposed to be a bit more careful and mindful of the landscape.'

'I'm sure you're right.'

'You were over there the other night, during the storm. Didn't you notice anything odd?'

'They hadn't started then because we'd only just arrived. Remember? They were just setting up their camping equipment. Maybe I should have another walk over there, and see for myself.'

'Yes, that's a great idea, Annette. It would be nice to have a second opinion.'

'Do you want to come with me? I feel a bit nervous walking into that situation alone. Assuming it is a situation, I mean.'

'Of course. There's safety in numbers,' Shelley said, weak with relief. At last, someone was taking her seriously.

Annette led Shelley along a path just

below the farmhouse.

'It goes straight across the islet,' she explained. 'Much quicker than going around by the beach.'

'I wish I'd known about that the other day,' Shelley said ruefully. 'Who gave the professor and his people permission to excavate on the islet?'

'I've no idea. They had the right papers. I know that much,' Annette said.

As they reached a spot parallel to the back corner of the farmhouse, Paris called from the terrace.

'Annette, Shelley — where are you going?'

'Don't tell him,' Shelley said in a whisper.

'Just for a walk and a bit of girlie chat,' Annette said, waving at him in a perfunctory manner.

'Shelley, I'd really like to talk to you,' Paris said. 'Please, come back for a moment.'

'I'm going for a walk with Annette,' Shelley said, her voice firm. It was not easy to refuse him. He looked so handsome standing there in the midday sun. Even from a distance she could see the light catching his lovely eyes. She waved and turned away from him, feeling a pang as she did so. It did not matter how much she loved him; he was up to no good, and he would not fool her again.

'I hear you two were getting close last night. What's happened since?' Annette asked.

'I told you, he was talking to Professor Grunwald. Obviously, the professor is comfortable enough with Paris to let the German accent drop.'

'Are you absolutely sure it was Paris?'

'I know it's hard for you to believe, Annette, but he was standing in the office doorway when I went into the hall, just after Grunwald left.' Shelley felt unaccountably guilty about being suspicious of Paris. Why she should, she did not know. But her resolve seemed to be slipping, the further away from the farmhouse they were.

'What exactly do you think they're up to, Shelley?'

'I think it has something to do with Nazi loot. Stefan said his father was shot stealing something, and his father's letter, which I've lost, mentioned a place called Helena's Bay. I think the bay where the Professor and his men are digging is Helena's Bay, though it's not called that on the map, is it?'

'It's too small to even have a name. Why Helena's?'

It did not occur to Shelley to wonder why Annette did not know Yaya's first name. 'Then there was something else. There was a website set up by Stefan's cousin, searching for family members, but when I went back to it the day after, the site had disappeared off the net.'

'That is strange.'

'I think that maybe it wasn't Stefan's cousin at all, but someone interested in knowing where Stefan's father hid the loot.' Shelley struggled to keep up with Annette's long stride. The path might have been a quicker way across the islet, but it was also rocky and uneven.

'Who do you think it might have been?'

'The professor and probably Paris. I told him — Paris — about the letters. Actually I told a few people. You were there, too, remember? It could have been anyone at the farmhouse, but it must have been Paris because Grunwald was in his office.'

Shelley stopped, the ache in her heart constricting her chest. She turned and looked back towards the farmhouse and beach. The ferry was still in, yet it should have been on its way back to the mainland.

'Someone broke into my room and stole the letters, and obviously went online to delete the website. Also, Mrs Caldicott and Miss Charters keep trying to stop me wandering off on my own. So I think they're involved, too. But maybe not. I mean they're nice ladies, aren't they? Truth is, I don't know who to trust.' She started walking again, catching up with Annette.

'Fancy Paris being caught up in this,' Annette remarked. 'I mean, I thought myself there was something odd going on, but not this. I've noticed that Paris and Mrs Caldicott are often huddled together. They're not meant to have met until this week, yet it's like they've known each other forever.'

'Yes,' Shelley said, nodding vigorously. 'I've noticed that, too. They had an argument the other day, and I heard her say to him 'Remember what I said'. I don't know what that was all about, but it suggests she's his boss or something.'

Once again, Shelley felt a pang of disloyalty. Yet, if they were involved in something illegal, and had hurt poor Stefan, she owed them no loyalty.

Still the memory of Paris's kiss made her lips tingle. His touch burned in her heart. He had been a very convincing lover. For the short time she was in his arms, she believed he really cared for her. That he wanted her, even. Perhaps he did, in a purely physical sense.

Whether he was a criminal or not, he would have the same needs as other men. He probably saw her as an enjoyable diversion, whilst he got on with the real job of finding whatever it was Stefan's father had stolen.

Paris's betrayal somehow felt worse than Tony's. Perhaps because her feelings for Paris were stronger. She pushed that thought aside.

'Don't worry, Shelley, we'll get to the bottom of it,' Annette said, breaking into her reverie. 'We'll soon be close to solving this.'

'The ferry is still in. Or at least it was when I just stopped by just a few moments ago. That's really rather odd, don't you think?'

'Not really. There were no passengers waiting, so the pilot sometimes waits a while. Or he could be making a delivery to the farmhouse. Come on, let's solve this mystery.'

Annette began to walk faster, making it even harder for Shelley to keep up. She wished she had worn her trainers rather than espadrilles. Following Annette was like going on a route march. The woman could certainly stretch her long legs. Shelley's shorter legs screamed at the exertion.

It took them nearly ten minutes to reach the other side of the islet, and approached the bay from a different direction to the one Shelley had taken. Annette took her through a small cut in some rocks, and just beyond it was the camp site, which Shelley had somehow failed to see two days before. Annette clambered down the rocks like a mountain goat, whilst Shelley followed gingerly.

Professor Grunwald, or whatever his real name was, looked up from his work and saw Annette. When he smiled, Shelley, who was still some way behind Annette, felt a jolt of fear. There was something in that smile. Something far too familiar.

'Hello,' Annette said. The way she said that one simple word was too confident. As if she was expected there.

'I've brought our young friend.'

'That's great. Bring her down,' Grunwald replied, in an English accent.

That was when Shelley realised how truly stupid she had been. She turned, ready to run back through the rocks, but stopped when she heard a heavy click.

'Stay where you are,' Grunwald said. 'We don't want to hurt you.'

She spun back towards the bay and saw him standing only a few feet away from her, holding a gun. Her heart flipped, then thumped violently. Her mouth felt arid, and though she tried to speak, to protest, she found she was unable to. Her mind screamed at her to run away, but her legs remained rooted to the spot.

'How much does she know?' Grunwald asked Annette.

'Pretty much everything. She's a lot smarter than she looks. Well, almost. She thought you were talking to the delectable Paris last night. He nearly found me in his office. Lucky that I managed to slip out through the window.'

'What have you done to Stefan?' Shelley asked, her voice breaking on the words.

'He's quite safe. We've taken him from the island,' said Grunwald, 'just as you thought we had.'

Shelley turned to Annette. 'You lied about what the ferryman said. He *did* tell you it was an old man.'

'Yes, I'm afraid he did. You're really rather easily fooled, you know.'

'What are you going to do to me?' she asked, looking at Grunwald, still aiming the gun in her direction.

'We're not killers, Shelley.'

'So why are you pointing a gun at me?'

'We have important work to do, and we can't afford for you to stop us. We're close to a breakthrough, thanks to the letters from Stefan's father. By the end of the day, we'll be gone, but you can't let them know what we're doing. We'll let you go as soon as we've found what we're looking for.'

'Did you set up the website, pretending to be cousin Bertha?'

'Yes, we did,' Annette said. 'I played Bertha, and sent pictures to Stefan to gain his trust. The website was a bit careless — we should have deleted it as soon as we'd made contact — but we were afraid that would alert Stefan. We used it to lure him here with the letters. But it turns out he did his own bit of investigating and found out Bertha didn't exist. That's why he rushed from the dining room that night. When he saw me arrive.

'We didn't know what he'd done with the letters till you blabbed to everyone the next morning. It was easy enough to go up into your room whilst you were in Yaya's class.'

'Are you Nazis?' Shelley asked.

Annette and Grunwald burst out laughing.

'No, we're not Nazis. We just like tracking down Nazi loot. There's a lot of it hidden out there.'

'I'm guessing you don't return it to the rightful owners.'

'Oh, get real, Shelley,' Grunwald said. 'There's hardly anyone left alive to claim it now. So why shouldn't we benefit?'

'Because it was stolen from people who then lost their lives to the Nazis. How can you even begin to enjoy spending money that's stained with the blood of innocent people?'

'Oh, I find it quite easy,' Annette said, grinning. 'No one cares any more, Shelley. Even if you reported us, we haven't broken any laws.'

'You've abducted an old man! And Grunwald or whatever his name is, is pointing a gun at me.'

'It's Greenwood,' the professor said. 'And as I've already told you, you'll be set free, as will Stefan, once we have what we want.'

'If you've hurt him in any way . . . '

'You'll what?' Annette snorted. 'Track us down? Seek revenge? We'll be long gone, my love, with enough money to ensure that we can stay hidden forever.'

'If I don't return to the farmhouse soon, they'll come looking for me.'

'No, they won't,' Annette said. 'You're out walking with me. I'm a trusted employee. And it's free time this afternoon, until supper at seven. No classes. No demonstration. They'll just think you're touring the islet with me. Now, be quiet, we've work to do.'

Greenwood called one of his men, and gave him the gun.

'Keep an eye on her.'

'What exactly are you looking for?' Shelley asked. 'Really, I'm interested.' She hoped that if she could keep them talking long enough someone from the farmhouse might worry about their absence. They might come looking for her. Then she remembered how cold she had been with the other guests, and with Paris in particular that morning. Why should anyone come looking for her? She had not encouraged their friendship, preferring her own company when she had any free time.

Annette sighed.

'You read the letter, didn't you? About the rubies? They used to be in the chalice at the old church. Then the Nazi occupiers stole them. Unfortunately they were then stolen back from the Nazis. By von Mueller senior and Helena. Yaya.'

'So when he said Helena's Bay, he wasn't talking about the name of the place. He was talking about it being her place. Her favourite place?'

'Yes, yes, something like that.' Annette rolled her eyes as if such details were of no consequence to her. 'Anyway, they stole them, and, we think, hid them here. He mentions this place in his letters all the time.'

'How did you know it was Helena's Bay?'

'That took some working out, but Yaya still comes here a lot, though she doesn't know why. She lost her memory when she got shot.'

'So why was Stefan von Mueller shot by the Allies if he was trying to help? And Helena?'

Annette sighed and put her hands on her hips.

'You're not that smart after all, are you? Stefan von Mueller senior and Helena weren't shot by the Allies. The Nazis shot them, several days after they stole back and hid the rubies. He died, but she managed to crawl away, despite her head injury.'

'So Stefan's dad did the honourable thing after all,' Shelley murmured. 'Does he know? Stefan junior, I mean.'

'Who cares?'

'I should think he does, very much. What have you done with him?'

'Annette!' Greenwood snapped. 'Why are you even talking to her? We've got work to do. This is sounding like the end of a Bond film, with you giving away the whole damn plot before she's supposed to die.'

Shelley gasped, her heart starting to pound in her chest again.

'You said you wouldn't hurt me.'

'And we won't. If you stop asking bloody questions. Now sit down on that

135

rock and shut up,' Greenwood said. He turned to Annette. 'Come on!'

'Hey,' the thug said. 'Where'd you get the gun?'

'Found it while we were digging,' Greenwood said, looking annoyed. As if he had not wanted Shelley to know that.

Shelley looked at the henchman, her mind racing. She did not know whether he was a killer or not. For all she knew, Greenwood was lying, and Stefan was already dead, and she would be dead soon.

'Do you know anything about it all?' she asked the man.

'Yeah, some. Now shut up.'

'How did Yaya . . . Helena . . . get away? If she was shot on the islet, she'd have nowhere to hide.' One thing she had learned from her experience with Tony is that criminals, especially when they fear no comebacks, do like to talk about how clever they have been.

'She wasn't shot on the islet, was she? She was shot on the mainland. Then she crawled to the hospital.'

'What was she doing on the mainland? I thought she lived here. The family owned the land before the Nazis came.'

'She did.' He rolled his eyes, as if Shelley had just said something ridiculous. 'But they caught up with them over there, near where they were building the extension to the church.'

'So how . . . ' Shelley stopped. She had been about to ask how the team knew that the rubies were still on the islet, but it occurred to her that might have them heading for the mainland, killing her on the way to stop her talking. The longer they were here, the more chance, she hoped, that someone would come and save her.

'What?' her captor demanded.

'How did she manage to crawl so far with a head injury?' Shelley had no idea where the hospital was, or even if it were right next door to the church, but it was the first question that she thought of to cover up her real query.

'How the hell should I know? Do I look like a brain surgeon?'

'No,' said Shelley truthfully, eyeing his stocky frame and cauliflower ears. 'No, you don't.'

The time passed by slowly. Shelley kept looking at her watch, but it seemed to her that the hands had stopped still. Other times she looked at it, when she was wondering when they might kill her, and the time seemed to have flown by.

She willed Paris to realise she was in danger. Or someone. Anyone. But as the minutes passed by, she realised they were not coming. No one cared.

'I'll tell you something else,' said the thug, after a long silence. 'When they got that Yaya to the hospital, turned out she was having a baby.'

'Paris's father?'

'Yep. And who had she been spending loads of time with?'

'Stefan von Mueller senior. You think Stefan junior and Paris's dad are half-brothers?'

'That's what Annette and Green-wood think.'

'Does Stefan know this?'

'Dunno.' He shrugged.

'So Stefan is Paris's uncle.' Shelley wondered how Stefan would feel about it. And Paris. He said his mother was Jewish. How would he feel, knowing that his grandfather was a Nazi, with all the implications that went with that revelation? But von Mueller had done the right thing in the end. He had helped Yaya hide the rubies — and it cost him his life.

Deep down, Shelley was not sure if a few rubies were worth the loss of a life. After all, they were only objects. While the money from them might be tempting for many, it did not make up for two boys — Stefan and Paris's father — growing up without a father in their lives.

As she sat there on the rocks, with the thug pointing a gun at her, Shelley began to think about her own life. Yes, Tony had conned her out of a lot of money. But she was still alive. She was young and fit, and had plenty of years ahead of her, assuming she got out of this awful situation.

Down on the beach, Annette and Greenwood were digging just inside a cove. They had clearly covered every inch of the bay, and this was the last place. What was the old saying about lost things? That you always find them in the last place you look? But they were not going to find the rubies there. Because Shelley was convinced that Stefan and Helena had not hidden them on the islet. They had hidden them on the mainland. And mainland Greece was a lot bigger than this islet. They would not begin to know where to look. Shelley had a good idea, though.

Despite not being personally interested in the rubies, she felt a glimmer of excitement at the thought of being the one to find them. Then they could be returned to their rightful owners. Maybe they would be able to rebuild the church on the islet. Except that apart from the visitors to Yaya's farmhouse, there was no one on the islet to attend it any more.

Before Shelley could even begin to worry about that, she realised she had to get herself out of the situation she was in.

8

Whilst Grunwald or Greenwood or whatever his name was and Annette dug alongside the other men for the treasure, Shelley eyed the thug watching her. Then she looked down at the ground, as if she had lost interest in him.

In fact she was thinking back to when she and her brother, Rob, were little, and visiting her grandparents for tea. Granddad always kept his war memorabilia in a case, out of harm's way, but one day, when he was cleaning it, he left the case open for a moment to answer the telephone. Immediately, Rob, who would have been about ten at the time, snatched up an old pistol that was her Granddad's pride and joy, swinging it around his finger like a sharp shooter.

Shelley had never seen Granddad angry before; he had always seemed such a mild-mannered man. But that day he was furious, slamming the phone down and grabbing the gun from Rob. He caught her brother by his shoulders and yelled at him.

'You stupid boy! Don't you ever do something like that again. You could have killed your sister. Good Lord, with a gun that old, you could have killed yourself, too.'

Rob had just stared up at him, wide-eyed with terror, whilst eight-year-old Shelley, in no way responsible for any of it, started crying.

When he calmed down, and after he had locked everything away safely again, Granddad pulled Rob and Shelley onto his knee.

'I'm sorry I frightened you, lad. It was my fault for leaving the case open, so I shouldn't have been so angry with you. It's just that if anything ever happened to either of you . . . ' To Shelley's amazement, her Granddad had tears in his eyes. 'I'd never forgive myself.'

He explained to them that the gun was a Luger and had been found on a beach. 'The sand and rain play havoc with the mechanism,' he explained. 'It erodes the firing pin. That means it could go off at any moment, either killing someone or tearing their fingers off. Chances are, it would do neither. If you fire a shot, it could just misfire and not hurt anyone, but you can't take a chance. All guns must be treated with respect. We think we're their masters, but with a machine that lethal, you can never take that for granted.'

As her reminiscence came to an end, Shelley dared to look up again. The gun the thug held was almost a replica of the one her granddad had owned. It had also been in the sand much longer, and had not been treated with the loving care that her granddad had given his.

Dare she take a chance and try to run? As irrational as it seemed; given that he might well try to kill her, she did not want to be responsible for him blowing his hand off. But if the gun misfired, then she might get a head start. Annette and Greenwood were way down on the beach, and she was younger and fitter than the flabby thug. Now she knew the shortcut across the islet, she might be able to outrun them all.

The main problem was that she would be running out in the open. While there were some hills on the islet, the path across the centre was in open countryside. There was no cover anywhere — apart from the few rocks at the top of the cliff on the eastern side.

As she thought about that, she looked up — and to her amazement saw Paris, hidden behind one of the rocks. He motioned to her to be quiet and pointed towards the bay. Stopping a cry that almost reached her throat, she stared resolutely at the beach. Her heart beat even more rapidly. He knew she was in danger. The fact that someone did made her feel much happier.

In the distance she saw a faint black

speck in the sky, drawing nearer and nearer. It was a helicopter! It swooped over the sea, and towards the beach, where it churned up sand, covering Annette and Greenwood, so that they could not see. The thug jumped up, and for a horrible moment, Shelley thought he might shoot her. Instead, he made a run for it up the cliff.

He had just got to the top, when a hand reached out and smacked him on the nose. The thug fell back a few feet, then raised the gun, and fired. Shelley screamed, but instead of the gun hitting Paris, it blew apart in the man's hand. Just as her granddad had said it would.

'Thank you, Granddad,' she whispered, vowing to give him a huge hug when next she saw him.

The helicopter dropped a ladder, which Shelley realised with some alarm she was supposed to climb up. She had never done anything like it in her life before, but she grabbed the ladder and, her shoulders aching with the strain, pulled herself up. She was aware of the chopper moving towards the top of the cliff, and a sudden tugging on the ladder. At first she thought it was the thug — but to her enormous relief it was Paris. He shouted above the roar of the chopper.

'Darling, don't climb, just hang on. It will take us to the farmhouse!'

It was the scariest, yet most exhilarating ride Shelley had ever had, flying over the countryside, clinging to the ladder for dear life.

Eventually, the helicopter hovered low enough for Paris and Shelley to alight. As soon as they were on the ground, she flung herself into his arms.

'Paris, I'm so sorry, I thought . . . '

To her delight he hugged her back just as enthusiastically.

'Darling, it doesn't matter. None of it matters. I'm just glad you're safe. The ferryman came to me. He said that even though his English isn't very good, he knew Annette had lied to you. It was an old man who got on the ferry the other day.' He kissed her. 'Come on, we need to get inside.' He took her hand and they ran the last few yards to the farmhouse.

The helicopter had landed in a field to the side of the farmhouse, and a good-looking young man of about Paris's age jumped out, and ran to them. As soon as they were all inside, Paris slammed the farmhouse door shut and bolted it.

'Thanks Dmitri,' Paris said, holding out his hand. 'I owe you one.'

'You are welcome, my friend,' Dmitri said. 'The police are on their way by boat. They say to keep everyone inside until they get here.'

Paris nodded, and they all went through to the sun lounge, where everyone was sitting looking tense and worried.

'Don't worry,' Len was saying to June. 'I've been in worse situations than this.' For the first time since Shelley had met him, he did not sound as if he was posturing, but making a real effort to put her mind at rest.

'It's odd about Annette stealing all the mobile phone chargers. Luckily they're all charging up again now.' His own mobile phone was in his hand, but attached by a wire to a wall socket. 'I wonder what their plans were.'

'Probably to leave us without means of contacting the mainland, while they escaped,' Shelley said. 'They'd probably cut the landline wires too.'

Everyone turned and beamed at her, and for a moment she felt the warm glow of people who cared about her welfare. To Shelley's utter surprise, Mrs Caldicott ran to her, enfolding her in caring arms.

'I'm so glad you're safe, dear,' she said warmly. 'It's all our fault. We should have . . . '

'Believed me? Oh, don't worry. With Stefan disappearing like that, I began to doubt myself.' Shelley laughed. But deep down she still felt the pain of their disbelief. Mrs Caldicott and Paris exchanged awkward glances.

'No, not that, Shelley,' Paris said, his

voice strained. 'We knew about Stefan all along. Or, at least, Mum did.'

'*Mum?*' Shelley's head was in a whirl. They had known? And what on earth did Paris's mum have to do with it?

'I'm Paris's mother,' Mrs Caldicott said. 'My real name is Rachel Georgiadis. Minnie and I have spent many years tracking down treasure stolen by the Nazis. To return it to its rightful owners, I hasten to add, or if not that, to at least give it to someone who can do good works with it.

'That was how I met Paris's father, nearly forty years ago. When we were investigating the loss of the rubies from the church here. We've never found them, by the way. It was something of a coincidence when we learned a few months ago that a rival team, not so interested in returning the loot, were also planning to come here and look for the Saint George rubies. We only came to keep an eye on them, and had no idea things were going to get so out of hand.'

'Just a minute,' Shelley said, her temper rising. She glared at Paris. 'You knew all along I was telling the truth?'

'Yes, but, darling . . . '

'Don't *but darling* me,' Shelley said, tears stinging her eyes. 'I . . . ' She floundered, overwhelmed by the enormity of it all. 'I can't believe you did that, knowing how . . . ' She ducked his outstretched arms, and moved to the other side of the room, where she fought to regain composure.

'We don't really have time for this,' Rachel Georgiadis said. 'I imagine Annette and her people will be along very soon. If we could get down to the ferry, we might be able to get away, but I don't know if there's enough time.'

'They've got a gun,' Paris said.

'It's an old one,' Shelley said, sounding like an automaton even to herself. She ignored Paris's entreating glance. 'A Luger. The firing pin has eroded in the sand. As far as I know, it's the only weapon they have. But just because it failed once, doesn't mean it will again. I don't know how many bullets are in it.' Shelley looked around the room, it just having occurred to her that someone was missing. 'Where's Yaya?'

'Yaya?' Paris looked around, too. 'I don't know. Mum?'

'I've not seen her for a while,' Rachel said. 'I thought she came with us.'

'She went to sort out some food for us all,' Len said. 'But that was a while ago.'

'You must find her,' Shelley said. 'Before they do. She knows where the rubies are.'

Rachel, Minnie and Paris exchanged glances.

'Does she?'

'Yes — she's been cleverer than anyone,' Shelley said. 'Pretending to lose her memory was a way of keeping them safe. In fact, they're exactly where they need to be. In the absence of there being a church on the islet any more. But if they get hold of her . . . '

Just as the words left her lips, a shout

152

came from outside. Everyone ran to the window, forgetting that there was a weapon involved.

Annette, Greenwood and their men stood in a semi-circle on the terrace. The thug who had watched Shelley was clutching his hand, which was wrapped in a makeshift bandage that appeared to have been torn from his T-shirt. Between them was Yaya, standing proud and erect, despite her great age and the fact that Greenwood had the Luger pointed at her head. Even if it misfired, it would injure Yaya, perhaps fatally.

Shelley put her hand on the latch of the French door leading out to the terrace.

'Shelley, what are you doing?' Paris said.

'I'm going to tell them where the rubies are.'

'What — are you on their side, or something?'

'No, I'm not,' she said, turning on him, her eyes flashing angrily. 'I'm on Yaya's side. Tony stole everything from me. My house, my bank account, even the twenty pounds I kept in a jar for when I ran out of bread in the middle of the week. But I'm still alive. And what that makes me realise is that money — the rubies — they're not worth anything if it means someone dies. They've already cost Stefan's father his life. And almost cost Yaya hers when she was shot in the head all those years ago. How many more lives have to be lost over those damn rubies? Len — ' Shelley ran across to the old policeman and, to his obvious surprise and delight, hugged him. 'It's been so good knowing you, Len. I hope we meet again one day.'

She went back to the window.

'I'll take Yaya's place,' she said.

'No! It's a lousy idea,' Paris said. 'I won't let you do this. If you take the ferry, they've got almost an entire hour in which they can torture you for the information, then they could just throw you over the side without a care.'

'No — listen, I can handle them. I

can keep them talking. They do like a chat — all of them.'

'You don't know if that will work. Look, I think your instincts about them might be a little off here.'

'Don't you dare tell me about my instincts, when you lied to me about them before,' she hissed, ignoring the shocked expressions in the room. 'It seems to me my instincts are pretty good. Your ethics, on the other hand, leave a lot to be desired.'

'What on earth is that supposed to mean?'

'Tony only stole my money,' she said, the tears she had tried to hold back filling her eyes. 'You . . . you tried to steal my sanity. Tried to get me to believe I was imagining things. Given the job you do, working with vulnerable people, I'd say that was pretty unethical.'

Paris stood back as if he had been slapped. His tanned skin turned pale.

'Then I'll just keep out of it,' he said, his face a mask of pain.

'Yes, do that. You've caused enough damage already with your secrets.'

Shelley, fighting with all her might to resist the urge to hold him and tell him she was sorry, opened the French doors, and went out onto the terrace.

'I know where the rubies are,' she said to Greenwood. 'Let Yaya go and I'll take you to them.'

'You're lying.'

'No, I'm not. I've worked it out. You could have, too, if you'd been a bit smarter. It would have saved you a week of digging at the very least.'

'Just tell us and we'll go there.'

'No, you have to take me with you. I . . . I want in,' said Shelley. 'I lost a lot of money because of a man, and I need it back. So you take me with you, cut me in, or I don't tell you.'

She tried not to imagine the horrified faces in the window behind her, and concentrated on fixing her face in the expression that Tony had always used when he'd lied most convincingly to her.

The door was still open, so the people in the farmhouse could hear everything she said, which made her feel ashamed of her behaviour. She dared not look back, or it would weaken her resolve. She told herself that it did not matter what Paris thought of her any more. But deep down, it did. As furious as she was with him, she wanted his approval.

Annette turned to Greenwood. 'She's telling the truth about that. Some bloke took her for everything she had.'

'What about her feelings for Paris?' Greenwood asked.

'What?' Shelley said. 'We had a bit of a kiss and a dance and he's supposed to be the love of my life? Hardly. Besides, he lied to me about Stefan. They knew the old guy had been here all along, and yet led me to believe I was imagining it. Even if I had feelings for him, which I don't, that fact alone would kill them completely. I want money. I want my life and my house and my bank account back. The best way to do that is to cut in on the rubies.' She looked at Greenwood levelly.

All the time she was talking, she was aware of Yaya looking at her with a level gaze. It proved to her that Yaya understood much more than she ever let on, including quite a bit of English.

'So,' Shelley said, 'Are you going to let the old woman go or not?'

'Yes, okay.' Greenwood pushed Yaya forward. As Yaya drew level with her, Shelley was sure she heard her whisper, 'You are a brave girl.'

Whether she had said it or not, it fortified Shelley for the task in hand.

Greenwood pointed the gun at Shelley and gestured her towards the road at the side of the farmhouse.

'Aren't we going by ferry?'

'What? And give them an hour to catch up with us?' Greenwood said with a derisive laugh. 'Oh, no, love, we'll do it in style — take the chopper.'

'Can you fly one?' Shelley asked, feeling more than a little worried for her life. She shoved her hand into the pocket of her Capri pants. Things were not quite going as she planned.

'Well, yes, otherwise I wouldn't suggest it,' he said, grinning. 'Come on.'

'You mean you're going to trust her,' Annette said. 'She's a good girl.' It was said in a sneering way, as though being good were a weakness. 'There's no way she'd get involved with anything like this.'

'I don't trust her. Not as far as I can throw her,' Greenwood said. 'But I do believe she knows where the rubies are. And if she doesn't, then I bet the boyfriend will give them up for her.' He turned to his henchmen. 'You three will have to take the ferry. There's no room in the chopper for us all.'

9

It was with some trepidation that Shelley sat in the chopper as it took off. Greenwood may well have flown one before, but he wasn't very good at it. It took him some time to get the engine going, then when he had managed that, the chopper swooped and swerved as he got it into the air.

Because he and Annette were concentrating so hard on keeping the chopper in the air, they did not see what Shelley saw. Which was everyone from the farmhouse running towards the three remaining henchmen, who had not yet reached the jetty, bearing all manner of brooms, pitchforks and other garden implements, with the feisty Yaya leading them into the fray. She noted, with relief, that Greenwood had given the Luger to Annette, who held it in her lap, meaning that the goons were unarmed and vastly outnumbered.

It took them a fraction of the time to get to the mainland that it would have on the ferry, which meant that Shelley had at least three quarters of an hour to keep Greenwood and Annette busy before help came. The folk left behind may well have contacted the police, but no one knew where she was going, and she was not prepared to give those details yet. She had one more bargain to make with Greenwood.

They landed in a field, just outside the town, and walked towards the centre. The hot sun shone on her head, and she felt her bare shoulders started to burn.

'I want Stefan to meet us,' Shelley demanded.

'No,' Greenwood said flatly. 'It's out of the question. If you're trying to stall us, lass, you can forget it.'

'You bring Stefan and show me he's safe or I won't tell you where the rubies are. Simple as that. Tell whoever is caring for him to meet us at the museum.' She gave Greenwood the name of the street in which the museum was situated.

'I know where it is,' he said. 'We went there when we were researching this job.'

'How do you know we haven't killed him?' Annette asked, smirking. Shelley measured her words carefully. Of them all, she felt that Annette probably was the most dangerous. The female of the species, and all that.

'Because I don't believe you're killers. Your goon was an idiot, who set off the gun by mistake. You could have killed me as soon as I realised your plans, but you didn't. You could have got the information out of Yaya, but you didn't. You could have forced me to tell you where the rubies were, then dropped me out of the helicopter, but you didn't.

'You're not very nice people, but as far as I know, the only person injured in all of this was your thug when he accidentally shot at Paris. So I think

162

that while you want riches, you'd rather it didn't bring a murder charge upon your heads. You might even think there's something romantic about the treasure hunting. I must admit I can see your point — except that despite you personally not having killed anyone, people have died for these rubies. Or, if not this, then Nazi loot very much like it.'

'You're a very clever lass,' Greenwood said, looking her up and down appreciatively. 'Pity you won't really be joining us. I never truly believed you would. Still, it would have been nice to have you along for the ride. You're quite a plausible liar for folk who don't know liars as well as I do. And you're young and pretty. Annette is getting past the age of being a femme fatale. You could open a lot of doors for us.'

Annette scowled.

'Bring Stefan to the museum and I'll tell you where the rubies are,' Shelley repeated calmly.

Greenwood made a phone call, after

which they all walked to the museum. They had been there about ten minutes when one of Greenwood's men arrived, walking alongside Stefan. The old man looked to be in reasonable shape. Shelley ran to him and threw her arms around his neck.

'Fraulein,' he said, sounding tired. 'It is good to see you again.'

'Are you okay?' she asked. 'Did they treat you all right?'

'Yes, they were good to me, all things being considered.' He held out his wrist, on which Shelley could see the imprint of a pair of handcuffs. Clearly the goon had realised they could not walk through the town like that, for which Shelley was grateful. 'They have fed and watered me, as they say. I gather you know where the rubies are.'

'In a minute,' Shelley said, estimating that it had been about half an hour since they left the islet. 'I want to show you something.' Before Greenwood or Annette could protest, Shelley ducked inside the museum, taking Stefan with her. She found her way back to the picture of Yaya and pointed to it.

'That's Helena. The girl from your father's letters. She still lives on the islet, where everyone calls her Yaya.'

Stefan nodded.

'She was very beautiful. And, from what I see here, with child.' He was clearly one step ahead of Shelley, judging by the sudden light in his eyes.

'I may be wrong about this, and forgive me if I am, but I believe the child she carried was your father's. Your half-brother. Which means you have a nephew. Paris.'

He nodded again.

'I believe you may be right.'

'There's something else,' Shelley said. 'Your father didn't die at the hands of the Allies. He died at the hands of the Germans. Because he was helping Helena to hide the rubies. He did the honourable thing, Stefan. That's what I wanted you to know. He may have had selfish reasons for doing it, because he loved Helena and wanted to impress her. But he still did the right thing. He stood up to those who would oppress the people here, and that's all that matters.'

Stefan's old eyes were moist with unshed tears.

'Yes, that is all that matters. Thank you, Fraulein. You have no idea how much this means to me.'

Shelley squeezed his hand.

'Okay, now the mawkish bit's over, can we get to the rubies?' Annette asked impatiently.

Shelley was not a violent person, but at that moment she felt like slapping the woman. Her blood ran cold when she felt the barrel of the Luger pressing into her spine.

'Greenwood might be enamoured of you, but I'm not. Now take us to the rubies, assuming you know where they are, and maybe we'll let you go.'

Shelley led them out of the museum. 'Come on,' she said, with more volume than was necessary. 'We're going to the church.'

Once they were inside its cool confines, she said, 'You're going to have quite a job getting them out.'

'What do you mean?' asked Greenwood, looking around as if the rubies might suddenly present themselves to him. 'Are they in the chalice?' He walked towards the altar. The sunlight from the stained glass window shone onto his white shirt, and once again Shelley saw the refracted red glow.

'Yaya — Helena — was very smart,' Shelley said. 'She and Stefan's father had already hidden the rubies when they were caught. I gather restoration work was being done on this church at the time, and that Yaya was part of the team who worked on it — stained glass being her speciality. She hid the rubies in plain sight.

'The shot to her head gave her the excuse to pretend amnesia. After all, who would argue with someone who had received such an injury? I don't know why she didn't tell the truth once the Germans had gone, but according to

Paris . . . ' Her voice faltered slightly on his name, 'There was some debate about who owned what, so perhaps she thought it best to keep them out of the government's hands. So that's what she did — ensuring that no one but she ever got close enough to them to realise.'

Stefan was looking up at the window. He smiled slowly.

'The rose,' he said. 'She made the rose out of the rubies.'

Annette spun round, looking up at the window. 'Oh, there's an easy way to get those,' she said, aiming the Luger at the window. Before she could do that, a figure rushed out of the shadows and knocked her to the ground.

'Oh, no, you don't!'

It was Paris! Shelley's heart flipped, and for a moment she forgot she was angry with him. Paris, who now held the Luger in one hand, held up a mobile phone with another. 'Good idea, Shelley, taking Len's mobile. We've been following your progress all the way here.'

He looked at her for a long moment,

and then looked away. Her heart sank, but she told herself it was for the best. It still hurt her that he had known about Stefan all along, yet had misled her, even asking all those prying questions about her life and her emotions.

Greenwood was about to make a run for it, when the doors of the church flung open and the local police came pouring in, led by Len. Greenwood and Annette were quickly put in handcuffs.

'Hey, pal, they chafe,' Greenwood said in an unexpected American accent. He looked at Shelley and winked. Despite the fact he was a complete crook, she could see some women would find him very appealing.

'I preferred the German accent,' she said.

'Did you? I kinda liked it, too. I based it on Hannes Messemer, from — '

'*The Great Escape*!' Shelley said, grinning. 'I knew it!' Her smile dropped when she saw Paris looking at her darkly.

Greenwood and Annette were led away. It was all over.

10

'How did you get across so quickly?' Shelley asked Paris. Stefan had gone with the police to give his statement, and Len, sensing that three was a crowd, had also left. They were alone in the church.

'Jet ski. Me and Len.'

'Oh! That's amazing,' Shelley said, smiling broadly. Then she remembered that she was angry with him, and he with her, and her face dropped again.

'Yaya told us we'd find you here.'

'Well, thanks for coming to save me.'

'Don't mention it. We wanted to be sure we got here before they took the rubies.'

'Yes, of course,' Shelley said. Suddenly feeling very tired, she sat down in a pew. It had been a long day, and her emotions had been as turbulent as the storm from a few days ago. She was aware of him taking the seat behind her.

'Paris, what I said. About you being unethical. I'm sorry. It wasn't a nice thing for me to say . . . But I don't understand why you did that, when you knew how much I was distrusting my own instincts.'

'You thought I was a crook.'

'Yes — but even then, only for good reasons. I thought perhaps you needed the money to keep the centre open all year. You . . . you hurt me.'

'I'm sorry. But I was only doing it to protect you. The thing is, Yaya told us at the beginning of the week that the rubies weren't on the islet. She didn't say where, just that Grunwald, Greenwood, whatever his name was, would never find them. So we just thought we'd let them get on with it.

'Only you insisted on investigating. I . . . we . . . were afraid you'd get hurt, so we thought the best way to keep you safe was for Annette and Greenwood to think that none of us believed you.'

Shelley jumped up again. 'For goodness'

sake, Paris. I'm not made of chocolate! And what about Stefan? He was abducted.'

'Mum found out where they were keeping him. In a rather nice hotel, actually. She managed to get a message to him through the chambermaid about our plans, and he sent one back agreeing to go along with them. We had him under surveillance all the time, so no one would have hurt him.'

'If you could tell Stefan about the rubies, why not me?'

'Because Yaya had kept her secret for over sixty years, and she insisted we did. She's spent sixty years not trusting anyone. She's family, Shelley — and what's more, she's our matriarch. We had to respect her wishes. You've no idea what trouble we all had, trying to stop you from blundering into a situation from which you might not escape.'

'Blundering? Excuse me. I think I've actually handled today pretty well.'

He looked up at her. 'Yes, you have. We shouldn't have underestimated you, and I'm sorry for that. You've been incredible today. The way you wrapped Greenwood around your finger, saving Yaya from harm, then taking Len's phone so we could follow your progress. It was very brave, and might I say, extremely sexy.'

'Paris, we're in church!' Shelley hissed. 'But go on . . . '

'What's the point?' he said. 'You made it quite clear how you felt about me. *Just a kiss and a dance.* If I'd known all you were looking for was a holiday fling . . . '

'I thought that's all you were interested in. That you might seduce one girl a week, and that I was just another notch on the bedpost.'

Paris stood up and began walking towards her.

'My darling, the majority of women who have come to the islet, until you, have been my mother's age. And as much as I love her, Oedipal I am not.'

'Well, then, I'm sure that you've got lots of girlfriends in London.'

'And you are attracted all too often to men who tell lies,' he said. He drew nearer to her, and for the second time in a few minutes she reminded herself they were in church and that she would probably go to hell for what she was thinking.

'What can I say?' She grinned. 'I can't resist a charming liar. But I could only . . . ' She stopped.

'You could only what?' Paris's hands caught her by her bare upper arms, pulling her close.

'We're in church,' she reminded him again.

'What better place to tell the truth?'

'After you. Did you really only come on the jet ski to save the rubies?'

'No, I couldn't care less about the rubies. I came to save the most precious jewel of all, and if I'd had a thousand ships, I'd have made them all come here. I may not be the love of your life, but I know you're the love of mine, and I hope one day you might love me. That is, if you can ever find it in your heart to forgive me for lying.

'I know it's only been a few days, but I do love you, Shelley. You're beautiful, you're clever, you're brave, and that whole combination, as I've already said, is incredibly sexy.'

'In that case,' she said, reaching up to press her lips against his, murmuring as she kissed him. 'I may well be attracted to charming liars, but I could only fall helplessly, hopelessly in love with the one who lied because he thought it would save my life.' She whispered against his ear, 'That is very sexy, too. Now I think we should leave the church before we both spend a million years in purgatory.'

Things got a bit hectic after that, leaving Shelley and Paris very little time to be alone. They both had to give detailed statements to the police, and all too soon the week ended, meaning that Shelley was forced to return home.

They phoned and emailed, but she feared that once the excitement of the situation abated, she might never see him again. It would not be easy, she pondered, to have a long-distance relationship with him living half the year in Greece, and half the year in London, whilst she still worked in Derbyshire.

One Friday morning, he called her at work.

'Can you get time off?'

'When?'

'Next week. We're giving everyone who was on the islet that week another free holiday, to make up for everything. But you can bring your mum, too. She'd be very welcome.'

'I'm not sure, Paris. It's costly and . . . ' Shelley had just put a deposit down on a new flat. It was only rented, but it was her first step to being independent again.

'I'll pay your fares.'

'I can't let you do that.'

'Of course you can. Like I said, we owe everyone a holiday. So I'm not just doing it for you.'

'Oh.' She felt a little disappointed by that, but said nothing. It was still a nice

176

gesture, whether he had paid for just hers or for everyone else's. 'Okay. I'll ask Mum.'

A week later, she set off from Greece with her mum, Pat. As they travelled, it occurred to Shelley that Pat had never had a proper holiday — yet she had spent her money on making sure Shelley had one.

'Mum, I'm sorry I've been such a pain lately,' Shelley said when they were on the plane. 'I really am grateful for all you've done.'

'You've nothing to apologise for, angel,' Pat replied. 'I'm only sorry I couldn't have stopped Tony from deceiving you.'

'Paris said we have to make our own mistakes.'

'Yes, and he's right. But that doesn't mean that I wouldn't do anything in the world to prevent you from being hurt. Doesn't matter how old you get, you'll always be my baby girl.'

Shelley reached over and kissed her mother's cheek.

'You'll love it on the islet. If anyone deserves this holiday it's you.'

When they arrived at the jetty, Shelley looked for Paris, but he was not there. His mother was waiting to welcome them. Shelley still had trouble thinking of her as anything other than Mrs Caldicott and even called her that when she stepped forward to give her a welcoming hug.

'Oh, sorry, I mean Mrs Georgiadis,' she said.

'I think you can call me Rachel now, dear,' Rachel said, kissing her on the cheek.

Shelley introduced her mother, and pretty soon the two women were chatting away like old friends as they all walked up to the farmhouse, trailing suitcases behind them.

'Everyone's here,' Rachel said. 'Minnie, Len, June, Stefan, and the rest.'

'Is Paris here?' Shelley said, trying to sound as nonchalant as possible.

'No, he had to take Yaya to the mainland yesterday to finish off some business. They'll be back tomorrow.' Seeing Shelley's disappointed face, Rachel said, 'He wouldn't have gone had it not been important. I know how much he wanted to see you. But all will become clear soon. Come on, let's go and get you two settled in. I hope you don't mind sharing a room, but with Stefan and a full complement of all the other guests from that week here, there was nowhere else but the huts, and Paris insisted he didn't want either of you sleeping in those.'

'No, that's fine, thanks,' Shelley said. She longed to see him, to hold him in her arms. The last few weeks of only being able to talk by phone had taken their toll, and she feared they might not recapture the passion they had felt when they were last together. A part of her wished that she were sharing his room — not that she said so to her mum or Rachel. Because there had been so much going on, and despite them both longing to be alone, the chance had not arisen the last time they were together.

As she unpacked, she began to worry that his enthusiasm for her had waned over the weeks. Yes, he had invited her to visit for a free holiday, but as he said, that was an offer made to everyone, not just her. It would have been odd had she not been invited.

She looked around the bedroom that was all as familiar as her own. They had moved a small bed into the room, so that she and her mother did not have to share the large double bed. Shelley opted to take the small one.

Pat had gone downstairs for a cup of tea. Shelley sat on her bed, which had been placed near the window, and looked out. She saw Len and June, the hairdresser, walking amongst the huts, hand in hand, clearly delighted to be together again. Rachel had told her that they had visited each other, and were talking of moving in together. She smiled sadly. She was glad they had found love, but her heart ached for Paris.

She was only able to get through the evening because everyone made such a fuss of her. She felt like part of an extended, loving family. Over dinner on the terrace, they all discussed what had happened. Pat was both enthralled and horrified by the story, especially when she heard how Shelley had dealt with it.

'Oh, it was very exciting,' Minnie Charters said. Shelley had since found out that was her real surname, and that Rachel had taken the name of Caldicott in honour of the two cricket-loving men in the film *The Lady Vanishes*. 'I haven't had so much fun since Rachel and I used to help Simon Wiesenthal hunt Nazis.' For once, no one doubted her story.

'I would like to hear about that one day,' Stefan said. He and Minnie also seemed to have hit it off. Shelley was glad. These were good people and they deserved to find happiness.

'It was nice of Paris to offer us this free break,' Len said, 'but actually there was no need. That's the most excitement I've had for years. I reckon you'd make a fortune here if you set up adventure holidays like that, Rachel.'

'What?' Shelley laughed. 'Invite people to be abducted and then fight treasure hunters?'

'It was brilliant though, wasn't it?' Len smiled, looking ten years younger.

'You were brilliant,' June said. 'The way you and Paris took off on the jet skis in pursuit! It was very sexy, Shelley. I wish you could have seen it.'

'Me, too,' Shelley smiled, trying to quell the ache in her heart for Paris.

'He'll be here soon, lass,' Len said, with a kindness that surprised her. She always thought of him as a gruff sort of man. 'Important doings afoot,' he said, tapping the side of his nose.

For a moment, Shelley felt annoyed that once again she seemed to be being kept out of the loop.

'I haven't had chance to explain to Shelley yet, but — ' Rachel started to say. Then her eyes alighted on something in the distance. 'Is that Dmitri's helicopter? I wonder what brings him here this late at night?'

Ten minutes later, there was a

commotion on the path at the side of the farmhouse, and Paris appeared at the corner.

'Shelley, you're here,' he said. 'Oh, Mum — can you go and help Yaya, please? I know we were supposed to stay another night, but . . . ' His eyes told Shelley and the smiling diners all they needed to know.

He took Shelley's hand and pulled her out of her seat. They ran down to the beach together, where he wrapped her in his arms and kissed her passionately.

'I'm sorry I wasn't here, darling,' he said huskily. 'I had to take Yaya on some urgent business. We were going to sleep on the mainland tonight and travel back on the ferry tomorrow, but I just couldn't wait yet another day before I saw you again . . . You look absolutely gorgeous.' He grinned.

'So do you!' she said, kissing him back. 'I was so afraid that you'd gone off me and that's why . . . '

'Never!' He stood back for a

moment. 'Why? Have you gone off me?'

'Never!'

'Then it's agreed. We're still help-lessly in love with each other.'

'Oh yes,' Shelley said, her heart swelling. Trying to compose herself, because she was aware they were still in view of the others, she asked him, 'What were you and Yaya doing?'

'Wonderful things. The rubies had to be moved once everyone knew where they were. We'd have had looters attacking the church all the time. The diocese have decided not just to give Yaya a medal for protecting them, but also talked the government into hand-ing back the islet to our family. Yaya asked the diocese to build a new church here and they agreed. We're laying the foundation stone tomorrow. That's why we've invited everyone. Also,' he paused a moment, pulling Shelley back into the closeness of his arms. 'Whilst it will take two years, and I can't possibly wait that long for you, I thought perhaps we could have our marriage blessed there, and maybe even christen our first child. What do you think?'

'You want to marry me?'

'Did you ever doubt it?'

'Then the answer is yes!' She threw her arms around his neck and kissed him. The sound of cheering flowed down from the terrace. Shelley hid her head in his neck.

'Perhaps one day then we can come and live here,' she suggested. 'I could work until we've saved up enough.'

'Darling, don't you realise?' Paris asked. 'It was never an issue of not affording it. It was only ever about the centre paying its own way. My family are hideously rich. We never have to go home again.'

Shelley gazed up at the farmhouse that she had come to love, and then back to the man she loved even more.

'Aren't we already home?'

He answered her with a kiss.